CAPISTRANO NIGHTS
Tales of a California Mission Town

BOOKS BY
CHARLES FRANCIS SAUNDERS

A Little Book of California Missions

AND CO-AUTHOR WITH
J. SMEATON CHASE

The California Padres and Their Missions

Polonia's wedding

CAPISTRANO NIGHTS

Tales of a California Mission Town

BY

CHARLES FRANCIS SAUNDERS

AND

FATHER ST. JOHN O'SULLIVAN

Pastor of Mission San Juan Capistrano, California

Illustrated by

CHARLES PERCY AUSTIN

ROBERT M. McBRIDE & COMPANY
NEW YORK   MCMXXX

First Published, April, 1930
Second Printing, August, 1930

CAPISTRANO NIGHTS

PRINTED IN THE UNITED STATES OF AMERICA

PREFATORY NOTE

San Juan Capistrano, the scene of the following stories, is a village of Orange County, California, situated on the main highway midway
between Los Angeles and San Diego. It lies in
the fork of two small streams, the San Juan and
the Trabuco, which issue from neighboring hills
and mingling their waters a little below the
town, flow together into the Pacific two miles
south.

The dominating feature of San Juan Capistrano is the old Franciscan Mission of the same
name, founded by that devoted pioneer missionary, Fray Junípero Serra, on All Saints' Day of
1776. At that time the region was populated for
miles around only by Indians, whose Christian-
izing and temporal betterment formed the ob-
ject of the mission's establishment, and continued to be the care of the missionary padres
for well on to sixty years, when the missions
throughout California were secularized by the
Mexican government, and the authority of the
missionaries came to an abrupt end. Then fol-

lowed years of neglect and vandalism, when
the Indians, a prey to disease and exploiting
whites, perished like flies; when the mission
buildings fell into ruin; and when the people
of San Juan Capistrano were often for long
periods without guidance of a resident pastor.
It is to this interim between the régime of the
old padres and the occupation of the mission by
Father O'Sullivan in 1910 that these stories
relate, the gathering of which has been quite
incidental to the Father's duties as a busy parish
priest — sparks, to use his own words, from the
anvil of his daily labors.

For the benefit of readers unacquainted with
Spanish, it will be as well to add here a few
hints for the pronunciation of the words and
proper names in that language, occurring in the
text:

Consonants may be pronounced as in English
with the following exceptions: *g* before *e* and *i*,
and *j* always, are like a strongly aspirated *h;*
h is always silent; *ll* in Spanish California is
like *y*, the sound of the *l* being submerged; *ñ*
is like our *ni* in *pinion; qu* is like *k; s* has always
its hissing sound, and *z* is like it, the lisp of
Castile having no vogue in California.

Vowels have the usual Continental pronunciation, and all are sounded (including final *e*) except the *u* in *gu* and *qu* before *e* and *i;* the *u*, however, is given its sound when surmounted by two dots, as *gü* = *goo.*

As to accentuation, words ending in a vowel or in *n* or *s* and family names ending in *ez* are usually accented on the syllable before the last; otherwise, on the final syllable. Exceptions are indicated by an accent mark upon the syllable to be emphasized. Diphthongs are considered as constituting a single syllable.

CONTENTS

ILLUSTRATIONS

CHAPTER ONE

OF THE OLD MISSION SAN JUAN CAPISTRANO. THE STORY OF THE BOY WHO WOULD MARRY, BUT CHANGED HIS MIND; AND OF THE GIRL WHO DID NOT CHANGE HERS. OF DOÑA POLONIA'S FIRST MARRIAGE, OF HOW SHE LED THE CHILDREN OUT TO PRAY FOR RAIN AND HAD TO BE RESCUED FROM THE FLOODS; AND HOW DOÑA MANUELA LOST AN EARRING WHICH SAN TIRADITO FOUND FOR HER.

ONE afternoon of a day in late November the train dropped me at San Juan Capistrano where I proposed spending a little while idling about the quiet precincts of the famous old Franciscan Mission that gives name to the village. Some years before I had been there and fallen under its spell. It was then without caretaker or inhabitant, its empty courts and corridors a prey to the whim of vagrant and vandal, save when a chance artist came there to paint and once or twice a month portly Padre José would come from San Luis Rey to say mass and hear confessions. Then the old *sala*, or reception room, which had been fitted up as a chapel, would be opened; there would be mass with sermon and music; and the Father, robed in cowled gown and cord of the Franciscan order to which he belonged, would lead his flock in procession along the crumbling corridors of the mission patio. Now, however, I had been told, a resident priest was there to give the place his entire attention.

I took my bag to the hotel, and from there a short walk brought me in front of the picturesque ruin to which earthquake, neglect and vandalism had reduced what was once the noblest of the mission churches. A coterie of irreverent goats, collected about a broken adobe wall, were briskly nosing out tidbits of straw and chaff. They looked up at me inquiringly, their shadows laid along the ground beside them in grotesque shapes. Other life was not visible, but from down the street came the sound of thumping balls and the cheerful calls of *rebote* players at their game. The declining sun was bringing out the magic of soft color on arch and pilaster and accentuating the ancient carvings with edges of purple shadow. In cracks of the desolated sanctuary's wall wild flowers had sunk their roots and were brightly blooming, fulfilling their immemorial rôle of comforters to the waste places; and high up under the broken eaves of the nave I could see that swallows had built their mud nests, row upon row. " An allegory, these habitations of the birds," thought I, " set in confidence and surety upon foundations consecrated to the divine "; and there came to my mind that lovely figure of Lanier's in " The Marshes of Glynn,"

> " *As the marsh hen secretly builds on the watery sod,*
> *Behold, I will build me a nest on the greatness of God.*"

Continuing my way, I passed beneath the *campanario*, with the four bells, each in its separate window, silhouetted against a clear sky, and reached the corridor-bordered front garden, where fancy pictures the gray-gowned Fathers walking in their time in the cool of the day and meditating among shrubs and flowers whose sweet fragrances breathed memories of the old home beside the Mediterranean — jasmines and gillyflowers and roses of Castile. None remained now, and all that spoke of the old padres' day were the worn stones and center post of a dismantled olive mill in the midst of

the plot. Some vines of a more recent caretaker's planting clambered lovingly about the
pillars of the corridor, where evidences of re-
pair work in progress were noticeable; then, entering the *zaguán* — the passageway piercing
the *convento* part of the building into the large
interior quadrangle — I encountered the new
padre himself, engaged in taking a photograph.
My interest in the mission and the mention of a
common friend or two gained me a hearty welcome.

" We are in a good deal of confusion here,"
he apologized, " trying to make the old quarters
habitable once more, a tedious job with the scant
help to be had, and so far there is only one bed-
room in readiness. There is a bed in it, and it
is yours if you will occupy it during your stay.
As for myself, I haven't been able to move in
yet, but am still rooming at Doña María's down
the street, where you must have supper with
me, and then we will return here and spend a
sociable evening."

" But," I demurred, " I have already regis-
tered at the hotel."

" Leave that to me," he replied, " I'll have
your bag over and you'll sleep here. And now,

if you will excuse me, I will go on with my photography; and if you want to take pictures, make yourself entirely at home. Remember, though, to give plenty of time; the light is dim in these corridors and going fast."

Such was my first meeting with Father O'Sullivan.

It was a cozy meal of country dishes, well seasoned with chile and garnished with ripe olives, that we had in Doña María's little dining room. Two of her intimates were there, pleasant-faced, low-voiced elderly ladies, whose family names, were I to give them, would be recognized as among the proudest of the old régime in Spanish California. The talk was in Spanish until they found that my unpracticed ear caused me to lose much, whereupon they would turn to English, which they spoke with accuracy but with evident reluctance. Supper over, the Father and I shortly took our leave with a *buenas noches* and an *hasta mañana si Dios quiere,* and returned to the Mission.

One of the refurbished rooms of the old edifice had been put in order for a living room. It was a quaint little apartment with a high ceiling of boards supported by rafters, and with two small embrasured windows. Niche-like insets in the thick adobe walls served for storing small articles. One was fitted with a set of worm-eaten shelves and a pair of wooden doors, while across the room stood an antiquated bookcase holding an assortment of ancient volumes mostly bound in sheepskin — sermons of Massillon and Bossuet, Padre Feyjoo's *Teatro Crítico Universal,* the works of St. Alphonsus de Liguri, and several well-thumbed breviaries in which the departed Fathers of the mission had said their daily office. In one corner a steep stairway led to the upper story. Of especial appeal to me, coming in from the night chill, was a delightful old fireplace of brick tile, smoked and blackened from long usage, for on the hearth a fire of olive wood cheerily glowed and sparkled. We drew our chairs up to it. As a tourist I had been guided perfunctorily about most of the missions of California, but tonight here I was in the privileged class of guest in the inner courts of the fairest jewel of them all, and I hugged myself for joy of it. The wind had arisen and was blowing gustily outside. It was just the sort of night for a chat by a friendly hearth.

" Many a night have I sat here alone," said the Father, " musing on the past and fancying I could read in the flames dancing up the chimney, or in the red coals dying in the ashes, the happenings of the mission's early years. Before this fireplace, I would think, the padres of old would draw up to warm themselves and confide to each other their aspirations and perplexities. Here, perhaps, they would plan their work, discuss its progress, even project other missions, and sketch out their ideas by the light of these burning logs. I could imagine Fray Juan Norberto de Santiago and Fray Vicente Fuster, of blessed memory both, talking over the construction of the great stone church begun in 1797 and nine long years a-building, amid whose ruins you stood this afternoon. I seemed to hear them weighing the merits of various samples of stone for arch, dome and pilaster, styles of ornamentation, the making of roof tile, the ratio of cactus juice to lime in the mixing of plaster for adobe walls; and there would, of course, be the perennial subject of the neophytes and their training. All these things, thought I, must have been talked over at this smoke-stained old fireside.

" Nor did I forget the sad nights hard upon

the tragedy of December 12, 1812, when
.the great edifice, the fruit of so much painstak-
ing thought and labor, toppled and was shat-
tered in a twinkling by an earthquake carrying
two score kneeling worshipers into eternity.
Could I not see dear Padre José Barona, after
having laid to rest the mortal remains of the
victims, sitting here by this same fireside, saying
his office in private and offering it up for the
poor souls that had been summoned without
warning into the presence of their Maker.
Without doubt the very breviary he read is still
among those books over there against the wall.
Thus intimately in my fancy did the old fireplace become woven into the Mission's eventful
history. Then one day as I was sitting in a
revery by the hearth, Juan Manriquez, of whom
I must tell you more later, walked in without
ceremony, sat down, spat on the floor and remarked casually, '*Padre Mut hizo esta chi-
menéa* — Father Mut made this fireplace.'
Imagine my chagrin, for it was fifty years or
more after the earthquake that Father Mut
first came to the mission! So did all those fireside fancies vanish in smoke."

Our talk being thus turned upon the mission's

history, in which we both had a consuming interest, the Father had much that was novel to tell me. The village of San Juan Capistrano at that time was still largely Californian of the early type. The inhabitants, while by no means all Spanish people, — for French, Basques, Indians, Mexicans, and some Germans as well as Americans were in the census, — were still predominantly tinctured with the old traditions, and Spanish was the principal language of the place. It prevailed wherever people congregated — at the post office, the grocery store, the blacksmith shop and the hotel, on the baseball field and in the handball alley. On Sundays at the mission chapel the sermon was in Spanish.

"All except a few American families," said the Father, "are Catholic, and from the child in arms to the old grandmother picking over the chile, you can find their baptisms entered in the mission records."

"And how do they all make a living?" I asked.

"Mainly from walnuts," he answered. "If you had been here a month ago, you would have found all San Juan, old and young, off in the walnut groves, *pizcando nueces,* as they say, picking walnuts. It is the big time of the year, when everybody is sure of making a little store of money out under the shady trees. Each grove has its hereditary pickers, who have grown from childhood to maturity gathering nuts in that particular orchard, and they expect to hand down the right of picking to their children after them. It is a sociable, pleasant occupation at one of the pleasantest times of the year, and entirely in line with every Californian's love of a picnic. San Juan Capistrano has not yet caught the fever of change and hurry that is infecting so much of California. We still ride horseback down here, or drive quietly about in the family buggy; neither have we any ' boosters ' nor ' For Sale ' signs. Nobody wants to sell anything but walnuts."

Here the Father anticipated a question that had been forming itself in my mind, and said,

" You may imagine that in an old-fashioned community of this kind there is a lot of unwritten history."

" Precisely," I returned, " but I can imagine, too, that it is locked up inside people who cannot or will not speak English."

" You are right, as I speedily found out.

When I arrived here something over three years ago, I was forced to realize that my first job was to learn Spanish. A working knowledge of that acquired, I found I had an open sesame to a storehouse of hidden treasure of a rather unusual sort. I was boarding at Doña María's and often of an evening as I sat at the supper table and she bustled in and out of the kitchen with *frijoles, carne con chile* and *arroz del país* [country rice] she would fall to talking of the old times. By and by, I began to think that what she was telling should be preserved, and as one's memory is treacherous, I got a notebook and would jot her stories down, just as they came from her lips, without embellishment on my part. In similar fashion I would note down things that others would tell as they came and went about the mission, and I am still at it. It may be that some of these jottings will amuse you."

With that the Father stepped to the bookcase and from one of the drawers withdrew a handful of small notebooks. " My *libritos,* the people call them — the little books."

Bringing them to the light he began thumbing them over. Presently he smiled.

" Listen to this," said he, and read as follows:

Once there were an old man and an old woman and they lived on a ranch and they had a son. And when the son grew up he wanted to get married to a neighbor's daughter who lived near by. So he told his father that he was going to marry.

" It is all right, son, that you get married," said the father, " but do you know what it is, this marrying? "

Said the boy to him, " No, I don't know."

" Well," said the father, " I am going to tell you what marriage is. Listen. In the morning it is water and wood; at noon it is wood and water; at night it is water and wood."

" *Pues ya!* " exclaimed the boy, " then I think I'll not get married! "

" ' But what a fright he had, the poor boy! ' remarked Doña María, who told me the story. And here is another matrimonial bit, where the male in the case seems not to have got off."

There came, so the story goes, a young man and a young woman to the padre to be married.

Said the padre to the girl, " What is your name? "

" María," she answered, " what else would it be? "

" And you have come to be married? "

" To be sure, padre, for what else? "

" And you want to be married now? "

" Now, padre, when else? "

" And with this young man? "

" *Válgame*, yes, with whom else? "

" Excellent! " said I, " terse and of the soil — real Hispanic salt. It suggests the humor of one of Shakespeare's rustics, or Hardy's."

" Now here," continued the Father, who had opened another book, " now here, while we are on the subject of marriage, is a bit that gives a glimpse of an old-time wedding. It was told me by Doña Polonia of her own wedding — her first, by the way, for she was three times married. I have it here in her own words."

" Ay, padre, when I was married to Francisco, my first husband, I was very young. Padre Rosales was then at the Mission, and Don Juan Forster and his family lived in it too. Francisco was a servant to Don Juan and lived in the adobe house where Jesús Aguilar lives now.

Doña Ysidora, the wife of Don Juan, said to me, ' Now, Polonia, when at the ceremony Francisco puts the three *reales* into your hand [1] and says, " I give thee these *reales* as a sign of marriage," and you say, " I receive these *reales* as a sign of marriage," whatever happens be sure you do not let them fall; be sure to hold them tight.' Well, during the ceremony, just as he gave them into my hand, Francisco's little brother who was standing near gave my hand a toss with his and I dropped the *reales!* It was an ill sign, padre, for did not poor Francisco die?

" There were many people there at the wedding; they came from far up the province, from Monterey and Santa Barbara and down near San Diego. The marriage took place in the old church, the one back of the mission which you must pass through the *zaguán* to reach — Father Serra's church, you know. In the doorway of the church the padre met us and asked the first questions: ' Francisco, wilt thou take Polonia here present for thy lawful wife according to the rite of our

---

[1] A present of money by the bridegroom to the bride would appear to have been a customary feature of the Spanish Californian marriage ceremony.

Holy Mother, the Church?' Then he asked me the same, and then we went farther into the church and joined hands. As soon as we did that the guns and small cannon that the men had got ready just outside the door went off, almost to deafen us, and the smoke came rolling into the church. And then we went up to the altar and mass was said, and we knelt under a large belt of flowers. Over my dress I had a white mantle of very fine silk, which covered my head also and hung down before my face. The only flowers I wore were three white roses in a row on the right side of my head. As we knelt we held large wax candles all covered with flowers. Six girls wearing crowns of white flowers stood with me and six with Francisco. For eight days there was merrymaking and feasting and then all returned to their homes. My great-grandmother gave me this advice: 'Polonia,' she said, 'if your husband says at midday it is midnight, you agree with him that it is midnight; and if at midnight he says it is midday, agree with him in that too!'"

"A famous adventure in which this Doña Polonia was a prime actor," the Father went on,

" and of which the people are fond of telling, is how she led the children in procession to pray for rain and all came home soaking wet.

" It seems that during the time when there was no priest living at San Juan, Doña Polonia, whose official duty was that of midwife, was also captain of the children of the pueblo. Whenever a child died, she it was who marshaled the little folk and saw to it that the two smaller bells in the *campanario* were properly jingled for the *angelito* (the little angel, as an infant that dies is still called), in order to typify the glad reception accorded the innocent soul upon its entrance into the joys of heaven. If the child was a boy, he was always dressed for burial as Saint Michael the Archangel, in a military uniform and with a little sword in his hand. Little ones served as pallbearers on such occasions, as they still do — boys for boys, girls for girls. The white coffin, the children dressed in white, carrying white flowers and singing ' Adiós, O Vírgen incomparable! ' made a pretty procession; but Doña Polonia would have the children carry little banners made of willow sticks almost a yard long, wrapped in white muslin with varicolored bandanna handkerchiefs flying at the top.

"Well, it happened in the eighteen nineties southern California suffered from a series of years of scanty rainfall. During one of these dry winters, when the *lomas* around San Juan were as brown as in midsummer, and cattle were dying of drought even in Trabuco and Mision Vieja cañons, the despairing ranchers counseled together and appealed to Doña Polonia to take the children out into the hills to pray for rain. Thereupon she had them make a *palanca,* or portable dais, with four handles formed by two poles fastened along the sides of the *palanca* and extending two in front and two at the back, in such a manner that the whole might be supported on the shoulders of four persons. On the dais they placed a niche draped in white muslin, with colored paper decorations pinned here and there, in the absence of the real flowers that the parched earth refused to yield; and in the niche were a crucifix and a picture of San Vicente. To the saint's picture they fastened little trophies among which was a pair of gold earrings. Some of the children carried willow sticks with other holy pictures attached to them, in the manner of placards.

There were processions on three days in succession. They formed at Doña Polonia's house, the long, dilapidated adobe beyond the tracks from the railway station, where the tiny chapel at the north end of the corridor is still in evidence. The first day they crossed the dry bed of the Trabuco to the west of the town and ascended the hill to the mesa that lies about a hundred feet above the arroyo; thence southward to Dana's Point (whence the hides were thrown down to the waiting *Pilgrim* in Dana's classic story) and home from the ocean by the back road. On the second day they proceeded northward into Trabuco cañon and returned over the *lomas* by much the same route as was trod by the soldiers of Portolá in 1769. The third day the procession moved eastward across the railroad and up the street past the Mission. On the way they had to pass the *cantina*, the town pool-hall and saloon, where a crowd of idlers in the corridor laughed at the motley procession wending its way in the glaring sunshine to pray heaven for rain, for it is well known that in this part of California it is the rule for a rain to give warning of its coming some days in advance. "Don't you mind them," said Doña Polonia; and on they faithfully trudged as far as the cemetery; then turning southward into the trail that follows the *lomas* and is visible from the Mission, the little procession was seen winding its way along, singing hymns and litanies and praying the rosary, that God might send the blessing of water upon the drought-stricken land. So to what is called *El Divisidero*, a ridge of hills which they followed in the southwesterly direction past *El Picacho*[1] towards the great opening in the *lomas* seaward, known as *La Boca de la Playa*, that is, *the Mouth of the Seashore*. Now, as they moved along *El Divisidero*, intent upon their devotions, dark clouds began to roll up in the south and a cool wind to blow from the southeast; and when the children drew near the beach, Doña Polonia marching triumphantly at their head, a heavy mist was falling which soon turned to drenching rain. The sky grew ominously dark, the wind increased in force, and rushing inland from the sea a *remolino*, or whirlwind, played havoc with the placards and San Vicente; so that the devoted little procession was thrown into confusion, and home three miles away! Meantime, in San Juan, as you may imagine, anxiety

[1] *El Picacho* is a rather high hill which rises in shape like a sugar loaf among the lomas near the ocean.

for the children's safety had risen with the
storm, until at last a rescue party was organized
and three large wagons were dispatched to *La
Boca de la Playa* in quest of them. It was a
water-soaked but jubilant little band, with Doña
Polonia in their midst, that drove into San Juan
an hour or two later; and ever since in dry
years, when prayers for rain are offered up, the
old people will nod their heads and say to one
another, ' Do you remember the time when Polonia led the children out to pray for rain and
had to be rescued from the floods? ' "

Here the Father paused to mend the fire
which was getting low. Then he resumed:

" On Saturdays it is customary for several
of the faithful women of the pueblo to come
to the mission with flowers for the altar and to
help Doña María put the sanctuary in order for
Sunday, as she has done since 1886. One Saturday not long ago, while they were busily sweep-
ing the tile floors, one of these, Doña Manuela
by name, came to me with a troubled look on
her face and said:

" ' Ay, padre, for a whole week now I have
lost the key to my little house and I don't know
where to find it. Last Saturday I started out to

come here with some flowers. I locked the door and hung the key on my wrist by its little chain. I passed through the corral behind Doña María's house. I laid it somewhere, I don't know where, and although I have prayed three Ave Marias every day to San Tiradito and promised a candle I have not found it.'

"Now, it happened that I had found a key with a chain to it the week before on the window-sill; so I said that perhaps I had it, and produced the key. Her eyes sparkled with delight and she exclaimed,

"'Ah, good San Tiradito, you have found it for me! How miraculous! How many things have you not found for me! See, padre, once my earring was lost for a whole week — *mi aril-lito*, which shone with the splendor of the sun. It was up at *Aguas Calientes*, where Elias lives, you know; they call it the Hot Springs now in English; but Don Miguel the Polish man lived there then — him they called Don Polaco. The grass was all yellow like my golden *arillito*, and so, though I searched every day for it, I could not find it. A woman told me a little Basque girl had picked it up but threw it away again. Oh, San Tiradito, how could I ever find it!

Every morning I looked by the arroyo's side
and every evening I looked along the road, and
prayed to my saint, but San Tiradito did not find
me my *arillito*. Then I would look again and
again and many times would I say, *San Tiradito,
dame mi arillito* (give me my earring). Then I
promised a candle to San Tiradito and looked
more and called again, *San Tiradito, dame mi
arillito, San Tiradito, dame mi arillito!* And
then, as I looked around, while the very words
were in my mouth, there in the yellow hay was
my *arillito!* San Tiradito had found it for me! '

"But," I asked, "who is San Tiradito? "

" ' Why, don't you know, padre? *Es un santo*
— he is a saint.'

"No," I confessed, " I'm sure I never heard
of him. There is none such in the calendar."

" ' But, indeed, padre, I don't know either
who he was, except that he has found many
things for me — many, many things that I have
lost he has found. Perhaps Doña Refugio
knows.'

"And she called Doña Refugio, who appeared
from the arched corridors, broom in hand. She
did know, and readily gave this account of him
whom we may call The Sonoran Saint Anthony,

for Saint Anthony, you know, is looked to with implicit confidence by the people to restore to them their lost articles.

"San Tiradito," said Doña Refugio, "was a poor man found dead near Guaymas in Sonora, and no one knew who he was. He was found in a narrow barranca where much cactus grew, and this concealed him so well that it is a wonder that he was ever seen at all. He had no friends, no one at all to pray for him, nor any relative to put a cross at his grave. But the Sonoreños felt a great pity for the poor, unknown soul, and gave him good Christian burial and set him a cross at the grave, but, of course, without a name. They had masses said for him, and the name they gave him was El Tiradito, the little castaway man, because he had, so to speak, been cast away [for that is what the word means]. And afterwards, whenever the people lost anything they would ask him to find it for them, and so they came to call him Saint Tiradito, for he would find things for them. Of a truth. Oh, yes, padre, I always burn a candle for good San Tiradito for he finds things for me when I have lost them.

"'*Mira,* padre,' exclaimed Doña Manuela, 'did I not tell you!'"

At the conclusion of this little story the Father arose, and wishing me a good night betook himself to his lodgings in the village, leaving me in solitary possession of the mission. Putting out the lamp and taking a lighted candle, I mounted the stairs to my chamber under the tiles. The wind had risen to a tempest, wildly banging loose doors and shutters, whistling through every crack and cranny in its career, and awakening ghostly sighs and moans throughout the rambling old ruin. It was a memorable night for me, abandoned thus to my thoughts, not a human being within call. Had I not been convinced that the spirits of the old padres of San Juan were secure in a better world, my imagination could easily have had them shuffling about this ancient scene of their labors and prying inquisitively into my wakeful face.

Dawn came at last, and with the returning sun the wind died away. When I stepped outside it was into a still morning of delicious serenity and crystal clearness.

CHAPTER TWO

Of Buried Treasure. How the Gardener Cozened Doña Eloisa out of a Mass. The Story of Elogio and how he Paid for a Jug of Aguardiente. The Story of the Oxen and the Treasure. Of Juan Manriquez and how he Sometimes Told the Truth.

THE taste the Father had given me of his *libritos* whetted my appetite for more, but it was not practicable for me at that time to remain another night at San Juan, and it was, indeed, some years before I was again at the mission.

On my return I found numerous changes. An adobe wall had been built enclosing the front garden, which was now a riot of cheerful bloom — marigolds, geraniums, verbenas, hollyhocks — and one lovely pathway bordered with the white trumpets of calla lilies led directly to the beautiful doorway of the old *sala*, where the visitors' register was and Lola, a dignified green parrot, sat on her perch and greeted me with a soft

" hello! " The Father I found now regularly
domiciled within, and eager to show all that
had been done since my former visit. Chiefest
and dearest to his heart was the restored Serra
church, the long adobe building that forms the
east side of the mission patio and has its name
from the fact that Father Junípero Serra
preached within its walls on several occasions.
This part of the mission had been in sad ruin
when I was there before, a lodging place for
bats and owls, but now it was carefully made
over in the original manner and a beautiful old
Spanish altar and *retablo* set in place. Near by,
a charming retired garden and fountain behind
the wall of the bells had been revived, while
the *convento* had been fitted up for comfortable
living. Such were some of the visible results of
the Father's thought and labor to call back what
might be possible of the olden glory of this
remarkable architectural achievement of the
Franciscan " conquest " in California.

After supper as we sat chatting, I said,

" You must have done quite a bit of digging
in the progress of this restoration work," and
added jokingly, " did your shovel ever encoun-
ter the old padres' treasure chest? "

The Father smiled.

"Do you know," he replied, "one of the most persistent notions in this neighborhood is that buried treasure exists about the mission. Some time ago Doña Eloisa, who lives in the village, came up to see me about something, and as she was leaving,

"'Padre,' she remarked, 'are you not afraid to be here in the mission at night?'

"'No,' said I, 'why should I?'"

"'Why, don't you know that people dig at night for money left in the ground by the old padres, and there are ghosts about?'

"'And did you know any of them?' I inquired.

"'Yes, indeed,' she replied, with a vigorous nod of her head, 'many. There was an old humbug — *un viejo embustero* — who used to live here and take care of the gardens in front, and beautiful gardens he had. He was a simple old soul, and worked for his bread only. God has repaid him, for he never received anything here for the work he did. He had come here from Mexico. Well, the old fellow got sick at last and was dying. I went to visit him one morning, and when he saw me come into the room, al-

though he had the death look on his face, he
turned his head and said to me, " So you have
come at last. Why didn't you come sooner? "
I was surprised for I had no reason to think he
wanted to see me. " Why," said I, " is there
something you want to say to me? " " Yes," he
said, " there is. I have something to tell you.
You know I have had care of the mission for a
long time. I have kept the gardens fresh with
flowers and the corridors well swept, and no
one has paid me a *real* except for the bread I
I have eaten. But, mind you, I have always
known where there was plenty of money within
reach. I used to take a coin now and then to buy
crackers and sweets at the store, but never much,
so it is nearly all there yet. Now listen to me.
Near the *zaguán*, which you pass through when
you go into the old church — the one they call
Father Serra's church — there is a pillar that
holds up the arch at the *zaguán*, and it has a
mark on it. It was put there very many years
ago with paint like they used for the decorations
in the big church that the earthquake ruined. Go
to that spot and dig beneath the mark and you
will find the money. I tell you because your
grandfather was *mayordomo* of the mission; and

the only reward I ask is that you have a mass said for my soul after I am dead." So I left him and that very afternoon I heard the bells tolling for his death.'

" ' And so you found the money? ' said I.

" ' Of a truth I did not,' she answered. ' You know the *zaguán,* just down the corridor there. I looked but I never could find any sign of a mark on any pillar near it; and afterwards at a confirmation they whitewashed all the pillars, so if there ever was a mark, it is a mark no longer.'

" ' But even so,' said I, ' why do you call the poor fellow an old humbug? '

" ' Because he was, padre; I don't believe he ever found a penny of any money at all, but made up the story to get the mass said! '

" ' Oh, it is indeed true, padre, this thing of buried money,' she went on. ' Do you know the sign of it? I will tell you. Where the money is hid there is a light comes out of the ground in the night, and rises straight up and then goes down into the ground again, *sube y baja.* When you see the light you must hurry and mark the place, so you can dig there the next day and get the money; for if you don't mark the spot instantly you can never find the exact place and the money stays in the ground. The old señora who was with me lately for a few weeks saw the light one night near the mission fence. There is no doubt but money is there somewhere, because the Verdugos once had a man working for them — his name was Marcelino Tabores — and one day, do you know, when he was digging a hole to put a fence post in he came upon money and began to put it in his pocket; but just then Pedro Verdugo came along, and the man quickly threw dirt into the hole and covered up the rest of the money. You see, padre, there must be money there.'

" In spite of Doña Eloisa's convictions," proceeded the Father, " I had my own ideas on the subject, and that afternoon I decided to take a look at the place where the old señora had seen her light. Sure enough, there was a piece of fence torn away, a wild tobacco plant, fifteen feet high, pulled up by the roots and lying near, and the ground round about disturbed in such a way as to show very plainly that a large hole had been dug there not long before. The earth had been thrown back and tamped down to make the spot appear natural, but close by lay the telltale, earth-stained jawbone of a horse freshly dug up from its resting place!

" Yes, indeed, hidden treasure is still a live subject at San Juan. And it is not only the old women of the parish who nurse the illusion. José Juan has told me of a man named Elogio, who lived by himself in a little old house back of the mission. It was years ago and this Elogio was a great drinker. Sometimes he would have some of his cronies in for a prolonged bout, and one night after such a debauch and they had drunk up everything drinkable in the house, Elogio said to the others, ' You wait while I go and get some more *aguardiente*.' But they all jeered at him. ' How can you get any more, with your money all spent and no credit? ' ' Never mind,' he said, ' you'll see; I'll get it.' So he went outdoors, and saddling his horse set off to the *cantina*, a jug in a barley sack tied to the pommel. On reaching the pueblo, as luck would have it, the horse stuck one foot into a hole in the road and fell, throwing Elogio over its head. Elogio picked himself up unhurt, and looking to see how it all happened saw the hole and in it an olla filled with money. Leaving it there untouched, Elogio went to the *cantina* and stepping up to the bar set down his jug upon it and ordered the *cantinero* to fill it with *aguardiente*. ' *Por qué, mocho?* ' said the *cantinero* (for *mocho* was Elogio's nickname, because he was without toes to one foot, the word meaning cut off or dehorned). ' What for, *mocho?* You haven't any money.' ' No money? What do you mean? ' said Elogio. ' I'll have you know I have plenty of money. You fill that jug.' Now Elogio was a big powerful man, and the *cantinero* was a little fellow; so he thought it prudent to do as he was told, and filled the jug to the neck. Thereupon Elogio dropped it into the sack, threw it across his horse's back, and swinging himself into the saddle, called to the *cantinero*, ' Come here, you little *gringo*, and get your money.' When the *cantinero* came out, Elogio reached down and taking him by the ear walked him alongside the horse until they came to the hole where the horse had stumbled and where the olla still was. ' There,' said Elogio, ' there's the price of your *aguardiente*, take it.' And with that away he galloped leaving the astonished *cantinero* standing over the olla full of money. He lifted it out of the hole, and without a word

" ELOGIO REACHED DOWN AND TAKING HIM BY THE EAR
WALKED HIM ALONGSIDE THE HORSE "

to anybody he left San Juan a few days later, a rich man."

" One day when I was having the garden behind the bells restored," the Father went on, " I was watching Damian Rios removing some earth with a scraper and a team of horses. Pete Lopez was helping and Phil Sullivan, house painter out of a job, was spreading earth along the mission wall. Said Damian in a stage whisper to Pete:

" ' *Si tropezamos con una olla y tiene mucho dinero, vamos á San Francisco, pero si tiene poco damos al padre* — If we strike a pot with a lot of money in it we go to San Francisco, but if there is only a little we give it to the padre.'

" ' Did the old padres have much money? ' I asked, to draw him out.

" ' To be sure they did. You see, padre, in those times every *ranchero* had to give a tenth of his cattle to the church. If he had a thousand head, a hundred went to the padre. My uncle Salvador Gutierrez collected the *diezmos* for Padre Rosales and I know.[1] And, padre, there

[1] There is a flaw in Salvador's reasoning, for it would seem the *rancheros* did not always make returns on the basis of fact. I have Father Rosales' account book of *diezmos* — that is, tithes — and the payments of cattle and horses are all

used to be an old man who lived in an adobe
house across the roac. in Stroschein's orchard.
He always rose very early in the morning while
it was still dark; and on Thursdays and Fridays
he would see a light come out of the ground here
beside this adobe wall next the graveyard. I dug
here myself twenty years ago, and do you know,
padre, the next night Doña Josefa de Romero
and Don Crisóstomo, the olla maker, were coming along the road and a marvel happened. They
saw a flame of fire shoot up from the place and
reach as high as the mission. So, you see, there
must have been treasure here. Another night
some people were digging here and while they
worked I sat on top of the adobe wall watching,
and while I watched, over there just by the
corner of the big church I saw as plain as could
be a padre dressed in his long *sotana*. I called
out to them, " There is the padre! " and they
all jumped up and looked where I told them,
but there was no padre there then.   But I had

methodically set down. If these records represent one tenth of
what the *rancheros* really owned, they must have been a
poverty-stricken lot, indeed, for some gave not a single head
during the three years when *diezmos* were collected at San
Juan Capistrano.
— *St. J. O'S.*

seen him in his cassock. It was *un espanto* — a ghost.' "

A famous background for hidden treasure tales is provided by the raid of Bouchard, the Argentinian pirate or *insurgente*, as they call him, who sailed along the California coast in 1818, robbing ranches and missions. One such tale is called *Los Bueyes y el Tesoro*, that is, *The Oxen and the Treasure*, and this is as the Father had it from the people:

Once there was a señor who got silver from a mine near Pasadena and San Pascual. All that is Pasadena now. In the inner room of his house he had bricks of silver, and besides that he had money that came in ships from Spain. The silver and the money he had covered up with raw hides. There were *onzas esquinadas*, the same as sixteen-dollar gold pieces; also five-dollar pieces, two-and-a-half dollar pieces, and one-dollar pieces, all of gold. *Onzas esquinadas* had five corners. *En el tiempo de los insurgentes* — In the time of the insurgents, as the Argentine and his crew were called — the señor decided to bury his money, for the churches were being robbed, and he was warned when the rebels would be coming. For two weeks he had in his back corral, to which there was a big door, two *carretas* with four yoke of oxen for each. Every day he went away and did not return until evening. He always had an Indian go with him. They went to San Pascual to dig holes, and took with them shovels and picks.

One day — it was in the month of November — the señor said, " When the evening star — *la estrella de la oración* — appears, commence to hitch up the oxen; and when the bells of the church ring for prayers for the dead [that is, at eight in the evening] that will be the sign to begin loading the *carretas*."

Now, the señor's wife was sick in the front room, and every night they passed through her room, the faithful Indian helping carry the boxes and *ollas* all covered with hides. When the *carretas* were loaded, bran sacks were bound upon the hoofs of the oxen, so they would not leave tracks. Then they started away, some Indians with them, and when the morning angelus bell was ringing (*cuando se tocaba el alba*) they came home again with the carts empty. So it happened that when the insurgents arrived, they did not steal anything, for all the rich people had hidden away their money.

Now, when the señor's wife got well, she said to him one day, " When are you going to tell me where you hid the money? " " I'll tell you some day," said he. So, one day, they took some lunch and rode horseback to the *cañada* where the pest-house is. They removed the saddles, and the señor said, " Let us have our lunch, and then rest." They were in a little flat, where there was a great oak tree; and while he was resting, his wife went to gather flowers, she said, but she really wanted to see if there was any loosened ground to be seen. When she returned, the señor was putting the saddles on the horses. " We are going," said he; " I fell asleep and dreamed, and according to the dream I ought not to tell you now where the money is. Some other time I will tell you." So they rode home, and a few months afterward the señor died, and neither the señor's wife nor anyone else has ever known where the place was where the money was hidden.

" A pretty puzzle forevermore," said I, " for dreamers and fortune tellers to juggle with. By the way, did the *insurgentes* actually raid San Juan Capistrano? "

" Yes," said the Father, " they rioted and caroused around for some days, but got little for

the reason that when they sailed from the north
country headed southward, a messenger was dispatched posthaste to warn the people. This gave
time for the Fathers at San Juan to pack in an
oxcart such valuables as would be tempting to
the pirates, and secrete them at a distance before
the raiders' arrival. The spot chosen was up the
cañon of the Trabuco, and the neophytes of the
mission used to maintain that after the pirates
had taken to their ships and sailed away and the
buried things were dug up, some were over-
looked. The hope of finding these things still
fires the fancies and stiffens the muscles of treasure seekers, but invariably to their disappoint-
ment.

" The same fevered brains that gave rise to
the stories of valuables buried and forgotten by
the padres of the mission, credited the Fathers
with possessing rich mines of silver and gold in
various parts of the country, where they were
said to go in time of need, as to a savings bank,
and draw their requirements. One of these hid-
ing places, according to popular belief, was in
Lucas cañon, and its existence was vouched for
by Juan Manriquez, a notable character now
long dead. He was a veteran of San Pascual

fight and about the last at San Juan to wear the picturesque garb of the old Californians. He used to swathe his head in a colorful bandanna and was an excellent replica of a moving picture pirate. Well, to get on with the story:

" ' For all of eleven years,' said he, ' I looked for the mine. That was many years ago when I was young and not like I am now, old and *rabiando* [complaining] and dead of hunger. The padres, in their time, took out lots of gold and made things for the mission churches; but nobody knew where the mines were, only a few of the oldest Indians, and they would not tell, for they never wanted anybody to know. There was one old rascal of an Indian — oh, rascal he was, and liar and deceiver — oh, the *aguardiente* I put down him, a flask every Saturday, as long as your arm, which cost me two dollars every time! He would never tell me where the mine was, but would bring me up Lucas cañon and say, " Look, search, and you will find it." And we would walk together, and I would look and break off stones, and he would laugh and say, " Look, search, and you will find it." Then he would hold up two fingers and say, " *Donde sale el sol y donde se mete* — where the sun rises and where it sets — there it is between, black above and yellow beneath and heavy, and not far away." How I walked and walked, dead of hunger and thirst, year after year, and never could I find the mine. He knew well enough where it was, and drank my brandy, but never once did he show me the place and say, " Here it is, this is the spot," but always it was, " Search, search, and you will find it." '

" It was this same Juan Manriquez," the Father proceeded, " who regaled me one day with this story of the Wicked Sacristan."

There was once an Indian sacristan named Tolquate at the mission. He knew where the padres kept their collection money and used to pilfer some of it when he got a chance. One day old Padre Barona was strolling along the corridor in deep meditation, and wishing to arouse himself from a drowsiness that had crept upon him, he took a pinch of snuff from the old square box he had brought from Spain, and putting the powder first to one nostril and then to the other, he gave out a sneeze of tremendous force. " *Véte, satanás* — Be off, Satan," he said. Walking a few steps farther and the snuff having crept farther up his nose, he emitted another sneeze yet stronger. " Begone, Satan, begone," again he ejaculated. By this time he was in the south corridor of the patio and the sacristan was over in the church dusting some statues of the saints, for that was part of his duties. Now, whether or no it was the sneeze that had startled him and shaken his hand, at any rate he did, by some unlucky accident, strike his hand against the head of one of the statues and sent it flying to the floor, where it rolled over and over, while from the broken head and neck silver coins poured out, scattering about the place. Tolquate rushed from the church and cried out, " Padre, padre, the saints have fallen to fighting among themselves and one has knocked another's head off." " Tut, tut," said the padre, " a fine story for a guilty fellow to make up." And calling two neophytes he told them to take the unfortunate Tolquate to the *carcel* and put him in irons, there to meditate upon his sins.[1]

---

[1] Juan Aguilar's version of Tolquate's adventure is that the sacristan climbed through the little high window on the east side of Father Serra's church, let himself down by means of a *reata*, and addressing the statue as " dark face and white heart," knocked its head off for telling on him. Then the money rolled out.

" Juan Manriquez was such a clever artist in words," remarked the Father, " that my suspicions became aroused as to his veracity. One day I questioned one of his cronies on this point. Tell me, I asked, does Juan Manriquez tell the truth? ' Oh, yes, padre,' he answered, ' Oh, yes, he tells the truth — sometimes! ' "

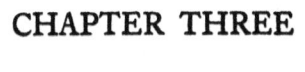

CHAPTER THREE

Of Acú, how he Sheared Sheep yet did not
get Rich, and how he told of Arrow-
making and other Aboriginal Matters.
The Strange Story of the Indian who Con-
tradicted the Padre; and another of the
Coyote who was not Himself.

T H E business that had brought me to San Juan proved to be not so promptly dispatched as I had expected, and I found an agreeable interlude in a daily visit to the mission, of which the Father had hospitably given me the freedom. One noon I entered the garden just as the angelus bell was sounding. The place was deserted except for the bell-ringer. He was a rather short, burly figure of a man with grizzled hair and a short tuft of beard, and with the characteristic lineaments of a California Indian. In the midst of his face was a nose of unusual width, forming a feature so distinctive as to be almost startling, and of his bushy eyebrows one was higher than the other. He wore a tall-crowned, frayed sombrero, faded blue overalls and an unbuttoned dark waistcoat, and having finished his duty with the bell, he stood for a moment head bowed and hat in hand. Then putting on his hat and deliberately coiling the rope-end on a nail, he crossed the garden, looking neither to the right nor to the left, and disappeared through the gate towards the village.

The picture of the old bell-ringer with his odd nose lingered in my mind the rest of the day, and when I made my customary call on the Father in the evening, I asked who the man was.

" Don't you know Acú? " he replied. " He has rung the mission bells this many a year, and a remarkable character he is. He is the last of the San Juaneño Indians hereabout — the Aháchamay people, as they call themselves. Like most Indians, he is reserved towards strangers, and as he speaks only Spanish and his own dialect, it is not possible for the casual visitor to get much out of him, though I have found him quite a mine of aboriginal lore and mission tradition. Our acquaintance began the morning after my arrival in San Juan. I was out for a walk in the sunshine and at the corner where the road to the railway station turns off from *el camino real,* I came face to face with him.

"'*Buenos dias, padre,*' he said, in a clear, bold voice.

"'*Buenos dias, señor,*' I returned.

"'*Soy José de Gracia Cruz* — I am José de Gracia Cruz,' he went on. 'I am sixty-two years old and was born here in this pueblo of San Juan. I have lived here all my life, and my father was born here also, before me. I know how to ring the mission bells for all the feast days of the year — for *Todos los Santos, las Ánimas, San Francisco, San Juan,* for *Nuestra Señora de Carmelo* — for all the great feasts of the year, padre. My father before me was bell-ringer, and he taught me how to ring the bells in the way they must be rung for each feast day.'

" This circumstantial account was confirmed by what I heard later from the town folk, to whom the man was colloquially known as Acú. One notable feature of his career that he failed to mention at our first meeting but which I afterwards learned about, was his part in the orchestra of Indians that used to play at the mission on feast days. Acú's instrument, it appears, was the flute. Of the violins Acú's father, Lázaro, played

one. Besides flute and violins the orchestra in-
cluded bass viols, *panderos* or tambourines, a
triangle and a couple of drums, and all were
played very softly when accompanying the
singers.

" Ay, padre," Doña Balbineda, one of my in-
formants would say, with a melancholy shake
of her head, " *qué buena música que había antes*
— what good music there was in the early
days! "

" As to Acú's flute playing, one of the town
gossips has told me that it came to an ignomini-
ous end in this wise: It seems that one evil day
Acú, stepping briskly from the corridor of the
village grocery, blowing lustily the while upon
his flute, unluckily missed his footing — it was
the wet season and there was much mud — and
the flute, flying from his hand, stuck deep in
the mire, where Acú himself fell sprawling.
Whether it was the disgrace of this public down-
fall, or whether the flute suffered a mortal hurt
from the accident, it is said to be a fact that its
plaintiff notes were never again heard in San
Juan.

" Quite as important as his rôle of flutist was
another that Acú filled for many years, that of

capitan of a sheep-shearing band from Rincon and Pala, which late in April was in the habit until recently of making the round of the various ranches, reenacting much the same sort of scenes as are described in 'Ramona.' He was a stout and faithful worker and invariably on good terms with the *rancheros* who employed him, a fact in which he took great pride, and which it pleased his vanity to advertise. '*Soy trasquilador número uno,*' he would boast, 'I am a number one shearer.' Driving into town of an evening in his little rattletrap of a wagon drawn by a bony nag, his big yellow dog, Oso, trotting behind, he never failed to salute his *patrones* — those who have at some time employed him — and stop, if they had the time to spare, to pass the time of day. '*Buenas tardes, patrón,*' he would say, in a voice that all the town could hear, ' Good afternoon, *patrón.*' '*Buenas tardes,* Acú,' would be the response. 'How do you do, *patrón?*' ' Quite well, Acú, and you? ' 'Very sad, *patrón.*' ' And why are you sad, Acú? ' 'Because, *patrón,* I am very old; also I am very poor, for God does not help me. I am now working these fifty years, and I have no money.' After which confession he would drop into ordinary chat and always with a compliment to the *patrón* for deigning to be seen in conversation with him. ' What would people say if they saw Don Juan talking with Acú! ' And then flipping the reins over his ancient Rosinante, he would move on, with the pleasing inner consciousness that he had made the town take notice of Don Juan's condescension to him.

" His lack of money, however, did not worry him seriously, for he had a certain philosophy regarding it that he explained to me one day.

" ' Padre,' said he, ' a thousand sheep at ten cents a sheep, how much is that? '

" ' A hundred dollars,' I replied.

" ' And fifteen hundred sheep at ten cents a sheep, how much is that, padre? '

" ' A hundred and fifty dollars.'

" ' Well, that is what I used to receive from my *patrón*, Luís Lartiga, who lived at Mision Vieja and had ten thousand sheep, and from Don Domingo Oyharzabal in San Mateo cañon, the one that goes up from the ocean down there beyond La Boca de la Playa. The ranch was called San Mateo, and the place where we sheared was *el Aguage de la Piedra* — the Water-hole of the Stone. I had from fifty to eighty shearers — Indians, Californians, all kinds of shearers. Acú, Indian — a good man, *quien sabe!* — was *capitán*. I got the shearers together and had them do the work and got their provisions. Flour and sugar were cheap. I spent twenty-five dollars a day for their meals, and gave then five cents a sheep for shearing. How much did that leave me, padre? '

" ' Fifty dollars,' said I at random. ' And still you are not rich, Acú; how is that? '

" ' Well, it is not good for an Indian to be rich, padre. There are not any rich Indians. It would not do, padre. A rich Indian is proud; he won't take orders from you or any American; but when all his money is gone, *es muy humildito* — he is very humble.'

" Acú is a true child of the mission," the Father continued, " linked with its very early history. His grandmother, he once told me, was one of the witnesses of the tragedy of 1812, when earthquake ruined the great stone church. She told him that there was an Indian boy in the church tower, ringing the bell for the next mass, for it was a feast day, when suddenly the tower began to rock. The boy was badly frightened and started down the stairway as fast as he could, when the tower fell in on him in one mass, and all was a chaos of ruin, with a great cloud of dust like a fog hanging over it.

" I always like to hear Acú tell about the customs and traditions of his people. What he says is generally worth while, and imparted often with a certain dry humor, as you may have noticed.

" One bright morning of early May, he came to the mission to ask for seed corn to plant. In addition I gave him the seeds from a large sunflower head, saved from the previous year.

" ' *Mirasol,*' he commented, giving me the Spanish name for it, as I shelled the seeds into a paper sack for him.

" Then I took him into the old *comedor*, or dining room, to show him the Indian relics that I had bought the day before from Charlie Mendelson, but without telling him of them in advance. The instant he saw them he stood stock still with surprise.

" ' I am going to take them away,' he exclaimed, ' they are my grandparents' things.'

" Then he began to tell me about them, giving me their names. The flat stones, the size of an ordinary washboard, are *metates*, or, in the aboriginal tongue, *no-ngo'-ha-la*. They used to grind acorns on them by means of a rubbing stone called a *mano*, or hand, which was often ten inches long, three wide and an inch thick. This was seized in both hands and rubbed back and forth over the acorn kernels spread upon the *metate*. The large mortar-like stones with a basin in them he called *morteros*, or in Indian, *no-tro'-pa*. They were used for pounding seeds in, with a round *mano*, or pestle. The *mano* for the *metate* he called in his native tongue *no'-mah'*, and that for the mortar, *ne-poy'-ay*.

" There were also three arrows, upon seeing which he asked,

" ' Who made these? '

" I told him Mesa had made them, a few weeks before he died.

" He examined every part of them, and then remarked of the feather tips,

" ' These are owl's feathers, they ought to be hawk's.'

" The arrows are in two parts, the point (which is about a third of the whole arrow) fitting into the shaft, which is of reed, as a finger fits into a thimble.

" ' This point,' he criticized with gravity, ' is willow, but *chamizo* is the right sort of wood to use. It is hard like iron and grows in the sierra. *O-út* is our name for it. See the *bréa* he put on this end of the point so it will stick tight in the reed. We called this *bréa,* or pitch, *hsant;* the arrow point we called *no-oo'-ka.* The whole arrow we called *hool.* The feathers at the end we called *mah-shat'.'*

" ' How did you say bow? " I inquired.

" ' *Pues, no me acuerdo* — indeed, I don't remember,' he answered, but an hour afterward he suddenly broke out.

" Now I remember what bow is in our language, it is *no-cour'-trip.'*

" ' Were the Indians good at using the bow and arrow? ' I asked.

" ' Good,' he answered. ' Indeed, yes. Why, an Indian could shoot from the other end of the patio (the patio is an acre in extent) and if the arrow only glanced you as you rode on horseback, it would knock you off the horse, and if it hit you it would go through you. I remember, when I was about ten years old, the *cimarrones* — that is what they called the wild Indians — used to come down from the Tejón and steal horses. Once they came through Cañon de los Negros to Temescal, where my grandparents lived, near where Corona is now, and killed four Indians who lived there and used to come here to San Juan to buy things. About twenty-five people of the country went after them to catch them. They overtook two, who stood their ground among the rocks at the place where Corona is. One of them received a bullet in his right arm so he could not use it. He had on his back a pouch made of deer hide in which he carried arrows, about ten. These he dumped out on the ground, and then lying down himself, he held the bow with his feet and shot at our men — shot even harder and farther than with his hands. But they finally killed him. The other one they caught alive and tied him to a tree to hang him. He raised his hand over his head, and pointing down at the top of his head, said, " *Diós, Diós.*" He wanted them to baptize him before they hanged him. But they didn't do it. They did wrong not to do it, didn't they, padre? They should have baptized him first.'

" Acú was frequently in a reminiscent mood when he was at the mission, and on another occasion he told me a strange story, which I will

give you in his own words. I have it here " —
and taking a notebook from a drawer, the Father
read as follows:

THE STORY OF THE MAN WHO CONTRADICTED
THE PADRE

Ah, padre, the *fiestas* the Indians used to have
when I was a boy at Temescal, the *rancheria* my
mother came from, over the mountains towards
Corona! Many would gather together in a circle
around a fire of thick logs burning in the center.
Everybody sang, each in turn, women and all;
according as their turn came in the row, they
would sing. The song was about the *gavilán,*
the hawk, and how he was caught and killed,
and how his wings were tied, and a thousand
other things they would sing about him.

One time when one Indian was singing — his
name was Pacífico, the *albañil,* or bricklayer,
who helped the padres with their building —
he forgot some of the song, which made him
ashamed, and to make up for having forgotten,
he said to the people:

" When the Lord walked in this world one
of our people was with Him, and when He

was crucified the Indian got some of His blood and kept it in the belt of his own *zapeta*, or breech-cloth. One day when the padre was in the mission preaching — it was a feast day — this one of our people was there, and while the padre was explaining what was done at the time of the crucifixion, this man spoke up in a loud voice and said: 'Padre, it did not happen that way, it happened another way.' Then the padre stopped and said to the Indian, 'Wait till after mass, I must speak to you.' So, after mass, the Indian waited, and the padre, when he came out, said to him, 'How do you know it happened differently with the Lord from what I said?' 'The way I know,' said the Indian, 'is because I was there and saw what happened.' 'Then how is it you have lived so long?' the padre asked him. 'I have lived all this time,' said he, 'because I have always carried some of the Lord's blood here in the belt of my *zapeta*.' 'Let me see it,' said the padre. So the Indian took out the blood from his *zapeta* to hand to the padre; but the moment it left the Indian's hand and the padre took it, the Indian sank down and became an old, old man, very old, all wrinkled up, as old as from the time of the Lord until now."

" You see," Acú added, in order to make sure
that the point of the story was not missed, " you
see, if the padre in the church sometimes forgets
what he has to say, was it any wonder that a
poor Indian should forget some of his song? "

" Acú, by the way," continued the Father,
" had times of being careless of his religious
duties, and one morning after a rather prolonged
absence from church he agreeably surprised me
by appearing at confession and communion.
Later in the day I saw him coming up the front
walk through the garden.

" ' *Buenas tardes*, Acú,' said I.

" ' *Buenas tardes*, padre,' he replied, " good
afternoon; but do you know, I am not Acú any
more, now.'

" ' I know it, you are another now, for Acú
used to stay away from confession.'

" ' Padre, did you ever hear about the two
coyotes? One said to the other, " Who am I,
what is my name? " And the other said, " You
are coyote." " No, I am not," said he. " You
are," said the other. " Let's see, then," said he.
" Do you see that house yonder where the children are? You run by there, and we shall see

who I am." So the other coyote ran by the house, and all the children cried out, " There goes a coyote! " Then he himself ran by, and the children cried out, " There goes another! " " Ah, don't you see," he then said, " I'm another." The same with me, padre; I am not Acú, I am another.'

" And there," concluded the Father, " you have somewhat of the history of Acú."

As I rose to leave, " there is one more thing you may tell me," I said, " I am curious to know how he came to be called Acú. You said he introduced himself to you as José de Gracia Cruz."

" That is a question I asked him once," the Father replied, " and the reason, as he gave it, is quite simple. It was a nickname his parents applied to him as a child. Coo, ah-coo, he would gurgle, learning to talk. So, Acú he came to be called."

CHAPTER FOUR

THE DEVOTION OF *EL MES DE MAYO*. HOW DOÑA DOLORES REMEMBERED AND PRAYED. THE STORY OF MATILDA, AND HOW SHE WALKED IN THE SPIRIT. THE LEGEND OF THE UNWILLING STATUE. OF THE DOGS' SAINT.

THE old mission stands, as for a century and a half it has stood, in a pleasant, sequestered, little valley opening to the sea, and backed by a half circle of those softly swelling hills the Spanish people call *lomas*. Their treeless slopes, brown with ripened grasses throughout the dry season, turn to vivid green under the winter rains, and one day of early spring, lifting your eyes to them, you see them flecked with color — blue and mauve, golden yellow and creamy white. Margarita, John Lobo's little daughter, will tell you the Blessed Virgin has been upon the hills walking, and that wild flowers have sprung up where her feet touched the earth. Go up and you will find it so — mats and runnels

of lupine and *cacomites* (as they call brodiæa),
owl's clover and shooting stars, wild pansies and
mustard and creamcups. And the air will be
sweet with their delicate perfume and musical
with the liquid call of the meadow lark, the
melody of the mocking bird and the droning of
foraging bees.

I had been upon one of the hills to watch the
sun sink into the Pacific, and on my reaching
the mission dusk was falling. I found the Father
before the gate surrounded by a group of excited children.

"Father, Father, you must punish Pablo,"
one of the little girls was saying with great vigor
and jumping up and down in her ardor, while
a boy's mischievous face looked impishly out
from around a near-by post. "He has been very
bad, Father; he found a *lechuza* in the cañon
today, and he killed *lechuza* with a stick, and he
brought the claws to school and frightened
us with them. He was very bad, Father, and
you must punish him; you must keep him
in after school tomorrow and make him say
doctrina."

"Well, well," said the Father consolingly,
"I must see about that," and after some com-

forting words to the little complainant, he turned to me and invited me inside.

"What is *lechuza?*" I asked as we walked across the garden.

"A barn owl," he replied. "You know those odd, monkey-faced birds that haunt the dark corners of barns and old buildings all over California? The mission was a paradise for them in the old days of its abandonment. By the way, have I ever given you the census of the mission's population when I first came here? No? Well, listen. First of all, there were spiders, the oldest inhabitants, and fleas, millions of them, the curse of the place; bats and owls (little Josefa's *lechuzas*), they were the ruin's faithful guardians, dozing on every rafter; mice, and lizards, of course, and *huicos* under every stone; snakes, tarantulas and centipedes; swallows that came and went with the seasons, like Arabs, and the white-throated swifts that lived in the cracks of the great stone ruin; bees and crickets, whom you may call the mission's minstrels; burrowing gophers and gypsy cats; snails, skunks, ants in myriads, and a few dogs! For a time I had a tent in the patio and would sleep there for the sake of the air, and sometimes of a night as I

lay on my cot I would see through the flaps a
coyote limping across the moonlit quadrangle
and silently disappear in the black shadow of
the corridors. And then the linnets! multitudes
of them, irreverent little birds that hopped on
my head at daybreak, and actually pulled at my
hair for nesting material! "

We were now in the mission patio, the large
inner quadrangle where in the early days of the
mission the Indian neophytes plied their various
trades — carpentering, blacksmithing, weaving
and so on — as in an outdoor workshop. I noticed that the children had followed us in. The
Father explained that there was to be a special
service in the Serra church that evening, in
which the children were to sing. He then left
me to make himself ready while I loitered in the
darkening enclosure. By and by the bells rang
out from the *campanario*, and it was not long
before I saw the shadowy forms of villagers
moving along the dim, ivy-hung corridors towards the church door, the women with their
heads enveloped in black *tápalos*, or shawls.
The church was dimly lighted except where the
candles lit up the beautiful altar. The service
was short, made up in part of the singing of

Alabanzas de María, or Praises of Mary, which consisted, as I remember, entirely of unaccompanied chants by the children, who sang alternately with chanters located in the body of the church, one group singing after another, the lovely music all the more appealing in the children's endearing treble. It was the devotion of *el Mes de Mayo* — the Month of May.

At the conclusion of the service the people lingered for a while in the corridor to pay their respects to the Father, who had a pleasant word for all; and as he and I finally walked toward his rooms we encountered outside the sacristy door Doña Dolores with her little granddaughter Sofía, waiting for Sofía's sister Ysidora. Waving her hand toward the crumbling arches, Doña Dolores said:

" Ay, padre, when I look at these old ruined walls that have no roof above them — *estos escombros* — I always think of the Indians who worked and built them, and I pray for their souls, that they may rest in peace. I was the youngest of my mother's children, and she died in 1884, quite old when she died. It was she told me how the Indians did the building work. She said they carried stones from the Mision

Vieja in *redas,* or nets, which they had made
out of coarse rope. The stone in the net would
hang high on the back, and the mouth of the
net would be over the head. That was the way
they would carry the stones, stooping over with
the stones high on their backs. Then two Indians would carry a big stone between them in a
net hanging from a stick or *palanca,* one Indian
before and one behind, each with the stick resting on his shoulder and the stone swinging in
the net between them. Long, long lines of
them, my mother said, stretched up the cañon
from the mission, all carrying stones. But for
the very heavy stones they would use oxcarts.

" There on the west side of the patio, my
mother said, was the *monjerio,* where the little
Indian and *mestizo* girls were kept in charge of
a woman. These were the *monjitas,* or little
nuns, as they were called. When my mother
was a little girl she often wanted to go and play
with them, but she could not get in for the high
wall. So she would gather some skulls of cows
that were lying about and make a pile of them
against the wall high enough to let her reach
the top of the fence, and then slide down the
other side holding to a rope which she tied to

one of the spikes that were fastened there to keep people out. So then she would play with the children.

" Beyond that side of the mission, there where the railroad is now, there used to be grapes and other kinds of fruit. I myself remember two tall date palms over there. And where the hotel is now there was a *tapeiste*, a kind of watchtower made of poles with a tule platform on top. The watchman was an Indian, José, or Chey, they called him, and he sat there all day, watching to see that no one came and stole the grapes. His main duty really was to scare the birds away by making a noise on a kind of drum. He wore only a *zapeta*, or breech-cloth. There he would sit all day long, playing a flute. But my mother knew how to get some grapes, and would creep along close to the adobe wall with the grapes hidden in her apron; and when she got to the front part of the mission, where she lived, she would feel safe and would hold up the grapes and shout, ' Chey,' and then run.

" Along this very corridor, padre, where we stand now, the old Indian women used to sit in a row, and pound up the olives to make olive oil for use in the sanctuary lamp. The olives were dried first like raisins, then pounded and put in a fine cloth, and hung up to drip the oil slowly. They would bring ollas of *atole* — that was a kind of corn gruel — to the old women while they worked. The poor Indians! When I see the old mission walls, I always say a prayer for them that their souls may rest in peace — *que sus almas descansen en paz. Buenas noches, padre. Buenas noches, señor.*"

As she moved away with the children, the Father asked me in to finish the evening with him, and he would tell me a curious story, connected with the church in the old days.

Starting a cheerful blaze in the little fireplace and pulling chairs up to it, he took a notebook from a drawer and opening it said:

" Here is the story just as I wrote it down several years ago when it was fresh in my mind, and you shall have it as I heard it."

And so he began this Story of Matilda and how she Walked in the Spirit:

It is mid-October. The nuts are nearly all picked and the *volantín,* or merry-go-round, is being put in place on the lot on the east side of the old plaza to gather in the walnut money from the San Juaneños. From my seat in the corridor I see old Crisanta coming toward the mission, eyeing as she comes the newly erected monument to Father Serra, and pausing every few steps to view some part of the building.

(" Let me interrupt the story here," said the Father, " to say, apropos of this old Indian Crisanta, that she once told Don Juan Aguilar that when she was a very little child both her parents died, and she lived alone in the mountains near Pala with her sister. They were like wild creatures, only going to their hut to sleep and roaming about the mountains all day in search of roots for food. When anyone came near them they would run off and hide. Juan's grandfather, Don Blas Aguilar, when looking up some cattle in the mountains, caught sight of the little Crisanta one day running wild, and thinking to take her back with him to San Juan Capistrano to find a home for her, he put after her on his horse, but had to lasso her in order to catch her. And so he brought her here to the mission and placed her with the Forsters. Well, to get on with the story — ")

After a few commonplaces and the present of a little sack of corn,

" Crisanta," I ask, " do you remember about the mission many years ago? "

" *Y como no* — and why not? " she answers, a little impatiently. " Did I not come here from Pala when I was eight years old and live in the mission? Don Juan Forster and Doña Ysadora were here then, and Padre Rosales lived in the rooms in front. Under the old chimney here was the padre's kitchen. Every week an Indian woman would come to stay eight days — she came on Sunday afternon and left on Monday the week after. She would work in the corner of the kitchen at the *metate*. I remember how I used to lean against this pillar and look into the kitchen and see them at work. The Indians used to bring *maíz* and *frijoles* and *chiles*, which they cooked for the padre. In the center of the room was the *horno* — the oven — and the *pretil* on which they used to cook. This *pretil* was like one of the brick benches out in the corridor. At first I did not want to eat their food, because at Pala we used to eat roots, and I thought the food they made here at the mission was not fit to eat."

As we walk about she points to the room on the west side — the corner room.

"There," she says, "was the *calabozo*, the lock-up. They would say to the Indians, 'if you don't mind me, I'll put you in there.' When I came here first, there were *gente* (Indians, she means) living in all parts of the mission; all these walls you see fallen now were good then, well roofed and had floors, and the corridor went all around with a roof on it. Why don't you fix it up again so people can live in it? You have plenty of money; you are very rich. Everything is fallen down now and *no sirve* — is no good."

We now stroll through the south corridor within the patio, where the ivy covers the columns, and at the first door of the Serra church Crisanta pauses, and putting her hand on the door turns to me and remarks:

"This is the door where the men went into the church. The women all stayed up front, and the men stayed back."

("And this," observed the Father in parentheses, "is the custom to this day.")

Passing around a heap of stones serving as a buttress to the east wall of the old church, we arrive at two small windows at the first of which, the one nearest the altar, Crisanta looks around and says simply,

" Just here, outside the window, they buried Matilda."

" Who was Matilda? " I ask, " and why did they bury her here? "

" Matilda," she replies, "was a young girl, the aunt of Acú, and she lived just across the road at the corner, there where that high poplar tree is, on the other side of the cemetery. She used to help the padre, doing the washing and ironing of the altar linens. One morning while he was saying mass, he saw her peeping in at him through this little window, and he turned his head several times to look at her, and some of the women in front also saw her. So that day, when the padre met her in the kitchen, he scolded her for looking in at the little window while he said mass; but she said she had not looked in at all. In a few days the padre and the women saw her again peeping in the window, and her brother-in-law saw her outside walking near the church. He said to himself, ' I'll scare her.' So when she came out toward the front where there were horses and wagons, he ran toward her to give her a good scare; but suddenly she disappeared. Then he went straight over to her house to find out what was the matter. He found Matilda in the house, ironing, and she said she had not been out. Another time the same brother-in-law saw her coming away from the little window, and when he went toward her she disappeared again. It was her spirit, padre, her *sombra*, which was walking about while she still lived, but it was a sign that she was going to die; for in a few days die she did, and the bells of the mission rang of themselves. Then the padre said she should be buried beside the window where she had peeped in during mass; and so it was."

"Afterwards," remarked the Father as he laid down the notebook, "I learned that the story of Matilda is well known in San Juan, and is told with some details that Crisanta had not mentioned. One day Acú spoke of her:

"'It is true, padre,' said he, 'that Matilda was my aunt. She lived near the mission in a house that stood over by that big tree at the corner of the lane. She was a very good girl, but some people had spoken ill things of her. You

see it was this way: the day she died the people
were expecting the bishop, and a Portuguese who
lived beyond the Trabuco heard the bells and
came down to find out if the bishop had arrived.
But it was not the bells of the mission at all that
had sounded; it was the bells in heaven ringing
to welcome the girl. Truly, padre, it was
heaven witnessing to the goodness of the girl
and rebuking those who had slandered her.
After that nobody ever said a word against her
name.'

" With respect to the bells, Doña Polonia
has a somewhat different version.

"'Padre,' she once said to me, 'when Matilda died the bells of the mission did, indeed,
ring of their own accord. No hand pulled the
rope, which remained coiled upon the peg while
they were ringing. It was very early in the
morning, and the father was writing at the time.
When he heard the bells he could not imagine
why they were ringing, and it made him angry
to think that somebody should be meddling
with them. So he sent Rafael, the sacristan, to
see who it was. Rafael came back and said the
rope was hanging in a coil from the peg on the
wall, but the small bells were ringing. Then

the news came that the girl had died that very hour.'

" And that, remarked the Father, " is the story of Matilda. There is another curious tradition of the mission, which may be called the Legend of the Unwilling Statue. It is short. Let me read it to you."

Many years ago, so the tradition runs, after the secularization and while there was no priest living at San Juan, the ruined mission was in charge of the Fathers at San Gabriel, who came and went at intervals. Now it occurred on one occasion to the padre at San Gabriel that it might be better if the statue of the Blessed Virgin in the mission at San Juan were taken to the safer quarters of Mission San Gabriel, and so he sent for it. There was a deal of sorrow in our little pueblo as the statue was borne away, quite a crowd following it in tears and lamentations.

Now, on the arrival at San Gabriel, a strange thing happened. When they attempted to put the statue in place, it would not stand up. Do what they might, it continually toppled over. Thereupon the San Gabriel priest, sensible man that he was, told the people to take it back to

San Juan, for it was evident beyond the shadow of a doubt that the Virgin was unwilling to have her statue removed from the original place.

So back went the statue. And now another marvel. Whereas when the people were carrying the statue from San Juan, it was so heavy that the carriers could hardly bear up under the weight of it, on the return it was so light that the carriers could run with it. You can imagine the rejoicing of the San Juan people, who turned out en masse when they heard that she was coming back and went to meet her as far as Los Alisos, nine miles up *el camino real*, as they call San Juan's main street.

I found a special interest in this story as a Californian variant of one that the traveler encounters in one form or another throughout Christendom. At its conclusion I arose to leave, when the Father said he would accompany me to the gate. In the village some dogs were barking.

" That reminds me," he observed, " of something Acú once told me about the dogs' saint. One day an errand took me to Acú's house, and the dogs came out with him to meet me.

" 'How many dogs have you, Acú?'

" 'They are not mine, padre; they are María's. She has four. Sometimes I say to her, 'María, why don't you get rid of some of these dogs?' And she says to me, ' *Pobrecitos perros,* the poor dogs, they too have their saint.'

" 'And who is he?' I inquired, quite curious.

" 'Why, San Lázaro — Saint Lazarus, to be sure.'"

What, indeed, more natural? For, when Lazarus sat at the door of Dives, did not the dogs come and lick his wounds?

CHAPTER FIVE

José Dóram Sings an Ancient Ballad. Somewhat of William the Fifth, his Verses
and his End. The Story of the Man who
Sold his Soul to the Devil yet Kept it.

.

IN accordance with the general pattern of old California towns San Juan Capistrano was originally built about a central plaza, the mission facing it on the north side. The planless encroachments of the American occupation gradually swallowed up this plaza until shops and houses now cover it entirely. Opposite what was formerly the northeast corner of it and about a hundred yards from the mission, there stands a tile-roofed house built in two parallel parts connected front and rear by adobe walls, so forming a patio or common yard for the families occupying the two wings. Above the roof rises, or did at the time of my visit, a chimney made of large mission roof tiles. The house has

a certain air of decayed gentility about it that
awakened my curiosity during one of my walks,
and that night I asked the Father if it had any
special history. The evening was mild and we
were sitting on one of the benches in the mission
corridor in order to enjoy the virgin freshness
of the night for a half hour or so. The mission
attendants had locked up and gone; Lola, the
parrot, head under wing, was asleep in her cage;
all was still except for the hum of passing traffic
on the adjoining highway and the village noises
mellowed by distance. Now and then a whiff of
musty perfume drifted in from the garden —
the delicious breath of the *huele de noche*, or
night jessamine.

"That was part of the mission establishment
in the early days," said the Father, "and is
commonly believed to have been the *mayordomo's* dwelling, and later that of Zeferino
Taroge, chanter of the mission. In the process
of secularization, probably under the tentative
scheme of disposing of the mission property and
forming a pueblo under Don Juan Bandini in
1841, it came to be owned by Don Blas Aguilar.
One evening some time ago, I had a pleasant
experience there."

I had been taking an after-supper stroll when I heard the notes of a guitar issuing from the south wing of the old habitation, where a light shone from within. The person playing was also singing in a low, sweet tone in Spanish. Entering the patio through a breach in the adobe wall, I knocked at the low doorway.

" *Pase*," came a voice, bidding me enter, and I stepped into a large room that served all the purposes of a dwelling for the little family inhabiting it. One glance left no doubt that it was built in mission times. There were the large square *ladrillos*, or tiles, forming the floor, on a level with the ground outside; the immensely thick adobe walls; the old-fashioned mission door with handwrought latch and hinges; the deep window; the low doorway leading into another room in the rear; and the fireplace in the corner with the chimney built diagonally across from wall to wall. Once inside, one might imagine oneself in a room of the mission itself. I found it to be the home of José Dóram and his wife Victoria, the *ahijada*, that is, goddaughter, of old Acú.

Supper was just over with a visiting friend and some children from the near-by houses —

Pichocha and Ernesto and Tomasito, each about
five years old. Everybody was still seated at
the table enjoying the songs of love and war
that José was singing to the accompaniment of
the guitar. He rose as I entered, and coming
forward bade me a grave but hearty welcome
in the manner of old California.

"*Es su casa, señor padre* — this is your
house, sir."

I begged him to continue his music, for, to
tell the truth, I had entered with the hope of
hearing a song of old San Juan, of which I had
been told there were several peculiar to the
place.

After a few commonplaces during the tuning
of the guitar, he began to sing. His manner was
deliberate and earnest, the tune a melodious
chant, and the accompaniment, while elaborate
and skillfully performed, was not in the least
overdemonstrative but blended harmoniously
with the voice. The song was called *El Clarín*
— " The Trumpet " — the farewell of a lover
called by the trumpet to battle and perhaps
death, begging of his beloved some memento
before he departs. When he had finished,

" Now," said he, " I shall sing you a song

that few know anything of at San Juan, for I
learned it when I was a very small boy, and
those who taught it to me are all dead and
gone; but before I begin I must relate the cir-
cumstances in which it was first sung or it would
have no meaning to you.

" In the early days there was a very rich man
who had a large grant of land from the King
of Spain on account of services he had rendered
as an officer in the king's army. He had many
cattle and servants. Among the servants was an
Indian who with his family lived quite near the
ranch house, and whom he favored by receiving familiarly into his house and extending to
him other marks of preference. A son was born
to this servant and the master stood godfather
for his child; and this, of course, drew the two
together closer than ever, for now they were
compadres. The rich man himself in time had a
child, a baby girl, and because the servant's son
was his *ahijado* — that is, his godson — the boy
was permitted, when big enough, to come and
play with the little girl. So the children grew
up together, and in time became lovers, but
when the father noticed that they would walk
together going on an errand, he forbade them to

do so. Nevertheless, they found a way to communicate with each other by means of notes placed in the hollow trunk of a willow tree. At last, when the rich man saw that his daughter was actually in love with the lad, who after all was only an Indian, he lost no time in separating them by sending the girl off to a distant part of the country, like up to Monterey, to live with some relatives of wealth and social standing, among whose acquaintances she would be likely to find a husband more suited to her position than the servant's son.

" Well, for quite a while she thought of nothing but her lover left on the ranch, the comrade of her childhood; but as time went on and no word passed between them, she began to take interest in the life around her, and at last when a suitor in her own station appeared she received him with favor; but her consent to marry him was given only on condition that the wedding should take place at her father's ranch, her old home. This was readily agreed to, and she and her *novio* with a great company of relatives made the journey together to her father's house, and shortly after their arrival the marriage took place. At the wedding feast there were songs and stories, the guitar passing from hand to hand amid great merriment. Now, when the instrument was placed in the bride's hands, she happened to look up toward the far end of the room, and there, standing in the crowded doorway among the servants and neighbors of humbler rank who were looking in, stood her childhood's lover. Then she leaned over the guitar and sang this song out of her heart, but none of the company knew what she meant except her old playmate standing there in the doorway. It is called *Los Recuerdos* — ' Memories.' "

Recuerdo, sí, á las horas de otro tiempo
  De mi partir, el doloroso dia,
  Tus ojos cual fúnebre cubrías
De tus mejillas triste y palidez.

Well do I remember the hours of another time, the unhappy day of my departing, the shadow of sorrow in your eyes, your cheeks pallid with grief.

Y nuestras almas tambien se encuentran puras
  En la grata mansion que el justo alcanza
  Pues ante el trono hallarás una esperanza
De un velo negro, fúnebre ataúd.

Our souls will chastely meet in the fair mansion that the just attain; then before the throne you will find a hope, from the tomb [released], the dark veil [rent].

Reconozco, sí, los troncos de esos sauces
  Ellos crecieron con tu amor y el mio,
  Tu frente lánguida inclínala al rio,
Ya no nos queda vida ni color.

I see again the trunks of those willows, they grew by your love and mine; your weary brow, lean it to the river; no longer is life ours nor brightness.

Siento en latir por siempre que me oprime,
  Siento un silencio cual fúnebre de muerte,
  Pues esto ha sido un caso de la suerte
Volver á vernos otra vez aquí!

Forever I am shaken with grief that oppresses me. I suffer a silence as of death. This indeed has been an act of fate, our meeting here again.

LOS RECVERDOS
(MEMORIES)

LOS RECVERDOS
(continued)

LOS RECVERDOS
(concluded)

man- si-on que el jus-to al-can-za Pues an-te el
cual fú- ne- bre de muer-te Pues es-to ha

tro- no ha-llar- as un' es-per- an- za
si- do un ca- so de la suer-te

De un ve-lo ne-gro fú-ne-bre a- ta- ud.
De vol-ver á ver-nos o-tra vez a- quí.

" Old-fashioned sentiment and comporting with the scene," said I, as the Father came to a stop, " but I find it depressing. I am beginning to feel as chilly as the poor bride."

" It is the night air," returned the Father, " let us go indoors. We'll have some fire and another sort of story — how William the Fifth died unshriven yet lies in holy ground."

When we were seated at the Father's cheerful hearth, he went on:

" This man I was speaking of, you must know, was a great rhymester, and though dead these many years, his verses continue to be repeated with relish by the old people hereabout. His father was of a good Spanish family, his mother an Indian, and his name was Guillermo Montalvar, though like some other artists before and since, he is best known by a *sobrenombre*, or nickname, in this case Guillermo Quinto, or as we would say in English, William the Fifth. He appears to have been of a sourish humor toward his fellow San Juaneños, to judge from a sardonic quatrain that I remember on village and saint:

Del santo nada se dice
  Porque el santo es santo y puro,
Pero de sus habitantes
  Son mas fuertes que un puro.

Of the saint is nothing to say,
  For the saint is a saint and pure, O.
But as for his congregation,
  They are ranker than a *puro!*

— that is, a strong cigar. One other that I remember, is of a kindlier sort, and enlists your
sympathies for the poor poet. It sounds like a
swan song:

Adiós, misión de San Juan,
  Con su pedazo de mar,
Donde no faltan enredos
  Ni lágrimas que llorar.

Adieu, San Juan, old mission, beside your
bit of sea, where troubles do not lack nor
tears to weep.

" Well, to get down to the real story about
him that I set out to tell you. I had it from one
of the old ladies of San Juan, that Doña Refu-

gio, of whom I have spoken before. This is as she told it:

" When I was a very little girl," she said, " there used to be an old *paisano* living here at San Juan whom they called Guillermo Quinto, that is, William the Fifth. He made the verses you have heard. A terrible drinker he was, and when he came to die he died without the sacraments, poor man. The padre at the mission refused him Christian burial, or to let him be put in the mission cemetery beside Father Serra's church. So his friends carried him to the hill a quarter mile east of the town and buried him there and put a cross at his grave. The cross, standing all alone up there on the solitary hill, used to be pointed out by mothers to their children, saying if they were naughty one of their punishments would be to be buried outside the *campo santo* in a remote place, as happened to William the Fifth. Then came *las viruelas* — the smallpox — in 1862. Ay, padre, that was a sad time! All day José Juan and his *compañeros* were digging graves. As many as nine died in a day, so that they even stopped ringing the bells at last when one died, for the tolling that never stopped could not be borne, and then the crying and the mourning in every house. Well, so many died that it became necessary to choose a place for a new cemetery. And do you know, the very hill where Guillermo Quinto lay was chosen for this, so that after all the poor man lies within holy ground."

" Good," said I, " give me stories with a comfortable ending! "

" Then there is another you will approve," returned the Father. " It was told me by Doña Rosa de Forbes, who had it from her mother in Sinaloa, but I have since learned it is a genuine old story of this neighborhood. Ninfa Serrano, who was born near El Toro and is now middle-aged, tells me she heard it as a child from her uncle Ruperto. It is curiously constructed on the pattern of our old nursery tale The House that Jack Built, and its name is *El Cuento de las doce Palabras Torneadas,* the story of the Twelve Turned-about Words. As its effect is dependent upon exact adherence to these words, it will be best for me to read it to you just as I took it down from Doña Rosa's lips."

With that the Father read as follows:

Once there was a man who had sold his soul to the devil for riches, and when the devil thought the time was up, he came for the man, and told him that he gave him so many days to arrange his affairs. Then the man became very sad, *muy triste*, and his wife, seeing him so, asked him the cause of his sadness. So he told her what had happened to him, for she had not known. Whereupon the wife, in order to console him, offered to go for him to the señor *cura*, the priest of the parish, to see if he could give some advice that would save the man from the clutches of the devil. So the señora went to the señor *cura*, and told him what was worrying her husband. Then the señor *cura* said there was only one way, and this was that her husband should know the twelve *palabras torneadas*, for the devil would be going to ask them, and if the man did not know them his soul was surely lost. Then she went and taught her husband the twelve turned-about words as she learned them from the señor *cura*.

Well, the devil came and sure enough said to him: " I am going to ask you some questions, and if you know how to answer them I shall let you go free." The man agreed, for he already knew the twelve words and was ready. Then began the devil:

"First of the turned-about words, you will tell me the one."

The man answered: "The holy house of Jerusalem."

Then the devil put the second question: "Of the twelve turned-about words you will tell me the two."

Answered the man: "The two tables of Moses and the holy house of Jerusalem."

Then asked the devil: "Of the twelve turned-about words you will tell me the three."

Answered the man: "The three Marys, the two tables of Moses and the holy house of Jerusalem."

Then asked the devil: "Of the twelve turned-about words you will tell me the four."

Answered the man: "The four evangelists, the three Marys, the two tables of Moses and the holy house of Jerusalem."

Then asked the devil: "Of the twelve turned-about words you will tell me the five."

Answered the man: "The five wounds of Christ, the four evangelists, the three Marys, the two tables of Moses and the holy house of Jerusalem."

Then the devil asked him: "Of the twelve turned-about words you will tell me the six."

Answered the man: "The six candles that burned in Galilee, the five wounds of Christ, the four evangelists, the three Marys, the two tables of Moses and the holy house of Jerusalem."

Then the devil asked him: "Of the twelve turned-about words you will tell me the seven."

Answered the man: "The seven gifts of the Holy Spirit, the six candles that burned in Galilee, the five wounds of Christ, the four evangelists, the three Marys, the two tables of Moses and the holy house of Jerusalem."

Then the devil asked him: "Of the twelve turned-about words you will tell me the eight."

Answered the man: "The eight choirs of angels, the seven gifts of the Holy Spirit, the six candles that burned in Galilee, the five wounds of Christ, the four evangelists, the three Marys, the two tables of Moses and the holy house of Jerusalem."

Then the devil asked him: "Of the twelve turned-about words you will tell me the nine."

Answered the man: " The nine months Mary carried her Son within her, the eight choirs of angels, the seven gifts of the Holy Spirit, the six candles that burned in Galilee, the five wounds of Christ, the four evangelists, the three Marys, the two tables of Moses and the holy house of Jerusalem."

Then the devil asked him: " Of the twelve turned-about words tell me the ten."

. Answered the man: " The ten command-ments, the nine months Mary carried her Son within her, the eight choirs of angels, the seven gifts of the Holy Spirit, the six candles that burned in Galilee, the five wounds of Christ, the four evangelists, the three Marys, the two tables of Moses and the holy house of Jerusalem."

Then the devil asked him: " Of the twelve turned-about words tell me the eleven."

Answered the man: " The eleven thousand virgins, the ten commandments, the nine months Mary carried her Son within her, the eight choirs of angels, the seven gifts of the Holy Spirit, the six candles that burned in Galilee, the five wounds of Christ, the four evangelists, the three Marys, the two tables of Moses and the holy house of Jerusalem."

Then the devil asked him: " Of the twelve turned-about words tell me the twelve."

Answered the man: " The twelve apostles, the eleven thousand virgins, the ten commandments, the nine months Mary carried her Son within her, the eight choirs of angels, the seven gifts of the Holy Spirit, the six candles that burned in Galilee, the five wounds of Christ, the four evangelists, the three Marys, the two tables of Moses and the holy house of Jerusalem."

Now the devil, seeing that the man had answered all these questions so well, began another list to see if he could not catch him yet; so he said to him: " Of the twelve turned-about words tell me the thirteenth."

Answered the man: " The thirteen thousand lightning strokes, may they split your heart! Get you gone, Satan! "

At this the devil made off and left the man free and repentant.

CHAPTER SIX

THE STROKE OF SAINT FRANCIS' CORD. DOÑA
MARÍA TELLS OF OLD TIMES AND HOW JOSÉ
ANTONIO MURILLO PAID HIS GRANDFATHER'S
DEBT OF A HORSE TO MISSION SAN GABRIEL. OF
PÁJARO CU AND THE BIRD OF FOUR HUNDRED
SONGS. THE STORY OF MARCOS MENDELSON'S
FOUR SACKS OF WOOL THAT WERE STOLEN AND
FOUND AGAIN. OF THE STARS THAT SHINE ON
SAN JUAN AND HOW THE PLEIADES CAME TO BE.

 **THE** following October the lure of the *libritos* took me again to San Juan and the Father's hospitable fireside in the old mission. As we sat there in leisurely talk the evening of my arrival, there came a patter of raindrops on the tiles without. It was the third day of the month.

"*El cordonazo de San Francisco*," observed the Father, "Saint Francis is striking about with his girdle."

I looked at him inquiringly.

"There is a Spanish dictionary at your elbow," he said, "turn up *cordonazo* and see what you find."

I opened the book and read:

Cordonazo, a stroke with a cord or rope. *Cordonazo de San Francisco,* a name given by the Spanish sailors to the autumnal equinox, on account of the storms which prevail about that time, or Saint Francis' day, the fourth of October.

" That same holds good in San Juan," the Father went on. " A year ago this day it rained, and Acú came into the mission, shaking the drops from his hat, and said to me,

" ' Do you know, padre, why it is raining today? It is because tomorrow is Saint Francis' day, and this is the *cordonazo de San Francisco* [the stroke of Saint Francis' cord]. This morning I was walking along the street and I met a woman going to pick walnuts. I said to her, " It is going to rain, for tomorrow is *el dia de San Francisco.*" " Oh," she said, " that used to be." She did not believe that it is the same still. But it is, isn't it, padre? You see how it is raining — it is Saint Francis striking with his girdle.' "

The Father added that he had asked Doña María about this saying, and her testimony was that a rain within the octave of the Feast of

Saint Francis invariably elicited the same comment from the older people. It would seem to be a bit of flotsam from the far-away days when the ships of Spain sailed this western coast.

"Doña María cherishes all such memories," said the Father, "and never tires of talking of the times *de muy antes*, as she terms the days of her girlhood. Not long ago she was telling me that the dwellings that today line the side of *el camino real* formed in old times one boundary of the little pueblo's great plaza, and made an excellent vantage point from which to watch the bullfights and other functions held there. On such festal occasions the corridors would be crowded with ladies in white mantillas, high combs and flounced skirts, admiring the horsemen in silk and velvet and glittering silver. The Californios, two or three generations ago, made a great account of silver, and were buttoned, buckled and spurred in it. In those days every ranch of consequence had its *platero*, or silversmith, whose handiwork adorned not only the hats, jackets and breeches of the riders, but the bridles, reins, bits and saddles of the horses as well. It was a brave sight when *caballeros* from

far and near gathered in the plaza of San Juan
and caracoled and galloped about it.

"'Good Christian times, too, those old times
were,' she is prone to say. 'One meeting you in
the morning greeted you with "*Buenos dias le
dé Diós; como pasó la noche?* — good day God
give you, and how did you pass the night?"
And you answered, "*Bien, gracias á Diós* —
well, thanks to God!" And during Christmas
week, when the cock crowed in the night, he
said, "*Cristo nació* — Christ was born!" but
nowadays what does he say? — "Dollar and a
ha-alf!"'"

"Modern inventions, in Doña María's view,
smack often of impiety. When the aeroplane was
first explained to her, she was obviously dis-
tressed.

"'*Quieren hacer más que Diós* — they want
to do more than God,' was her comment.

"As for wireless telegraphy, there could be
but one explanation for it:

"'*Hay diablos ya,*' she said simply, 'there
are devils still.'

"To the railway, however, she has become
reconciled, since the trains have been running
through San Juan these many years, and have

become an inseparable part in the scheme of things. Nevertheless, she will tell you with humorous sympathy of the old Indian, who, on seeing his first locomotive, exclaimed,

"' *Cuidado, tatita Diós, te van á ganar los americanos* — take care, grandpapa God, they are going to get ahead of you, the Americans! '

"When she was a little girl she lived with her parents on the Rancho Las Bolsas, which is still known by that name, except the part now covered by the town of Huntington Beach where a forest of oil derricks marks the plain that was once the grazing ground of the cattle of Don José Antonio Murillo, Doña María's father, and owner of the *rancho*. The other evening after supper she told a story that she said she had often heard her parents relate. It seems they once had a young man working for them as a *vaquero* whose duty it was every morning to leave the house early on horseback to attend the cattle. One morning a little while after he had ridden off as usual, the family were surprised to see him returning, holding fast to the pommel of the saddle and in a dazed condition of mind. He was, in fact, so helpless that he had to be assisted from the horse, when he was put to bed until the stupor wore off. At last when he was able to speak, Don José asked him what had happened to him to bring him home in that condition; but the young man steadfastly refused to tell.

"The next morning, finding himself pretty well recovered, he set out again for the day's work; but again, just as on the morning before, back he came in a little while, swaying in the saddle and quite helpless, so that they had to take him indoors and lay him on the bed. When he came to, he still refused to tell what had occurred. For several successive mornings the same strange thing happened, each time the horse bringing back the stupefied rider clinging to the pommel of the saddle, where the *reata* still hung; and each time Don José's efforts to elicit an explanation were unavailing. Finally, under a threat of chastisement if he did not make a clean breast of the affair, the young fellow confessed that the cause of the trouble was this: No sooner had he ridden a short distance from the house, he said, than a man would suddenly appear at his side, and struggling at one of the stirrups, would act as if trying to mount into the saddle with him. Thereupon such a terror would seize the youth that his senses would leave him and he would become as if dead, remembering nothing more until he came to in the bed.

" Then Don José, after thinking the matter over, said to the *vaquero*, who was really hardly more than a boy, ' This is what you must do. Ride out tomorrow morning as usual, and when the man appears to you, instantly turn away your head so as not to look him in the face and say: *Por parte de Diós, te pido si eres de este mundo ó del otro, y díme quien eres.* (In the name of God, I ask you if you are of this world or the other, and tell me who you are.) Then when he answers, you say to him: *No me des las gracias* (do not thank me), because it is not good to receive thanks in a case such as this.'

" So the next morning shortly after breakfast, the *vaquero* rode away as arranged; but it was not long before he was back again in the same dazed state as before. As soon as the family saw him coming they hurried out to meet him and helped him indoors and to bed. When he came to his senses he said that he had not gone far when the same man appeared as on previous occasions and tried to get up into the saddle, just as though it were not already occupied, whereupon the *vaquero* did what Don José had instructed him to do, turned away his head so as to avoid the man's face and asked: *Por parte de Diós, te pido si eres de este mundo ó del otro?* And the man answered in a voice that sounded as though it came from a big, hollow gourd: *Soy José Antonio Nieto, y debo un caballo á la Misión San Gabriel.* (I am José Antonio Nieto, and I owe a horse to the Mission of San Gabriel.) Then, added the *vaquero*, there was just time to say: *No me des las gracias,* when he lost consciousness, and all was black until he found himself stretched out upon the bed with the family around him.

"Now, you must know that this José Antonio Nieto was the maternal grandfather of Don José, Doña María's father, though the *vaquero* did not know it at that time; and so the very next morning Don José had his horse saddled and riding out into the pasture where his *manada*, or herd of horses, were grazing, he selected the finest one of all, and set out at once leading it to the Mission San Gabriel. There he turned it over to the padre in charge with the explanation that his grandfather José Antonio Nieto owed the horse to the mission and he had come to satisfy the debt. And from that day on, the story goes, the apparition ceased and the young *vaquero* was not troubled again."

" It was Doña María," the Father went on, after giving me time to digest this honest tale, " it was Doña María who first cleared up for me the reason for that strange expression *pá-jaro cu* — you pronounce it *pah' haro coo* — used in San Juan to denominate a thankless person. This is the Story of Pájaro Cu as she told it:

" There was a bird that had no feathers, and it was named Cu — in Spanish, *el pájaro cu*. This bird was engaged to be married to *la paloma*, the dove. Tecolote, the ground owl, proposed to all the birds that each contribute something to put clothes on Cu. So each bird gave a feather, and Cu had plenty of clothes. But, *mira*, when he was all dressed, away he flew and never came back. And now the dove is always calling for him, saying, *cu, cu*. Tecolote, too, calls for him, saying, *cu-cú, cu-cú*.

" The story would seem to be of Indian origin, for Acú knows of the bird Cu, and has given me a

version, which he calls — The Story of Cucúmel."

" Once there was a bird called Cu, and it had
no feathers, no covering of any kind on its body,
all naked. The other birds called a council and
decided to take up a collection for the naked
bird. Each one gave a feather. Then when the
bird was all clothed with feathers, it flew away
to the place where the sun goes down. When it
did not come back, its mate set out to look for
it, calling its name, Cu, Cu, Cu, Cu. It has never
found Cu, for it is still looking, and calling Cu.
So the Indians call the bird Cucúmel.

" Another bird story Doña María likes to tell
is about the *cenzontle*. That word, too, was a
puzzle until I found out that she meant the
mocking bird. As a matter of fact, in the speech
of the Spanish Californians, words 'not infre-
quently occur that you will search for in vain in
the ordinary Spanish dictionary. They are, indeed, not Castilian but survivals from the Na-
huatl, or language of the Aztecs, and have come
up from Mexico in the mouths of the people.
Cenzontle is one of these, and I find it of more

than ordinary interest; for its literal significance is ' bird of four hundred songs,' rather a pretty compliment to this well-beloved songster. Well, this is Doña María's story about it:

" ' The cenzontle,' said she, ' is the bird most faithful to his *esposa* or wife, and when she is on the nest caring for their little ones, he has to be singing always in the neighborhood of the nest so that she will not be sad, for she is *muy zelosa*, very jealous. But she does not sing while he is on the nest and she is off. Why? Because, she being so jealous, he can trust her.' "

Returning to the subject of old times and ancient customs, the Father remarked,

" You know the old Mendelson House, do you not, on the east side of the old plaza? "

I did — a long, wooden, two-story hotel, of a kind of architecture current in California seventy years ago. There were verandas, front and back, on both the lower and the second stories. Upon these the rooms opened, and an outside stairway gave access to the upper floor. The building still stands, with little change of outward aspect, but it now calls itself the Hotel Mission Inn.

" The founder of this hostelry, which flour-
ished notably during the early American occupation," continued the Father, " was one Max
Mendelson, whose given name sounded so
harshly upon the ears of the San Juaneños that
they soon turned it into one more to their liking,
to wit, Marcos. This Marcos Mendelson not
only conducted a hotel, but also dealt in mis-
cellaneous merchandise, and a story is told of
how he once lost four sacks of wool and regained
them in a most unusual manner. It seems that
in those days the men of San Juan followed an
old custom of Spanish countries and dealt
roughly with Judas in effigy on *Sábado de gloria*,
as Holy Saturday was called. During the pre-
ceding night movable articles of every description, such as wagons, plows and harrows, would
be brought in front of the mission from various
places (without the formality of securing the
owner's permission), and would be strung out
one after another in a long procession extending
from the mission's big front entrance, or *zaguán*,
far down *el camino real*, a distance of perhaps
a third of a mile. Seated in a wagon at the head
of the caravan would be Judas, an ungainly cari-
cature, the body made of an old suit of work

clothes stuffed with *malva* (a weed that grew abundantly at that time of the year), a collar and tie about the neck, and on his head a wide-brimmed sombrero. As a finishing touch, in the upper left-hand, outside pocket of the coat would be his will, providing for distribution of all his worldly goods and chattels to his lawful heirs. The settlement of the estate would be accomplished after mass, the *misa de gloria*, by the owners of the alienated property coming and claiming it, which they would do with many uncomplimentary remarks, you may be sure, about the testator and his administrators. The final act in the comedy would be to lift Judas from his seat in the wagon, set him astride a bull, brought in the night before, and then start him on a wild ride to the ranges of Mision Vieja ranch, whence the animal had come.

"Well, early one Holy Saturday morning, Señor Aguilar, who told me the story, was walking past Mendelson's hotel and store, and was surprised to see Marcos pacing the corridor in evident distress of mind. 'What is the matter?' asked Aguilar. 'Matter enough,' replied Marcos. 'Four sacks of wool that were in my yard were stolen last night — gone and not a trace

of the thief.' 'Take heart,' said Aguilar, 'perhaps I can help you catch the robber, for not
more than an hour ago I saw a man driving a
wagon with four sacks of wool in it, and a hard-
looking character he was, too.' 'Where did you
see him, tell me? ' said Mendelson in great ex-
citement. 'In front of the mission,' replied
Aguilar. 'He had stopped there, and it may be
you will find him there yet if you hurry.' Whereupon Mendelson set off toward the mission on
a run and there, sure enough, were his four sacks
of wool piled behind Judas in the wagon; and
sticking out from Judas' pocket was his last will
and testament, containing this clause: To my
beloved son, Marcos Mendelson, I leave four
sacks of wool."

When I took my leave that night the Father
accompanied me to the outer corridor. Saint
Francis' *cordonazo* had brought down nothing
more than a sprinkle, and the stars were shining
brightly. As I glanced up at them, the Father
remarked:

" San Juan has its peculiar ideas of astronomy
as well as of ornithology. The Great Bear, for
instance, is *el Carro Triunfal*, the Chariot Triumphal in which Elias was carried up into the

heavens; the Milky Way is *el Camino de San-tiago*, the Highway of Saint James; two stars in the southern part of the Milky Way are *los Oji-tos de Santa Lucía*, the Little Eyes of Saint Lucy, patroness of the eyes; *los Tres Reyes*, the Three Kings, are the three stars in Orion's belt. The first star to appear in the west after sunset is *la Estrella de la Oración*, the Star of Prayer, and is the signal to repeat the angelus when one is so far away that the angelus bell cannot be heard. Among the old San Juaneños it marked a definite time in the twenty-four hours, and as such entered into their common vocabulary. *Lo haré á la estrella de la oracion* was a promise to do something at the day's close, akin to the New Englander's old time locution 'early candle light.' The Pleiades are *las Siete Cabrillas*, a phrase inherited, in part at least, from Spain, but with a local significance given by Indian legend. There are differing versions of the story. Old Juan Robles says that the seven stars were origi-nally the seven 'affinities' of the wildcat. The coyote, having killed the wildcat, cooked the car-cass and fed tidbits of it to the girls, and then derided them for having eaten their lover, whereupon they turned themselves into stars, leaving this world of deceitfulness and shame far beneath them forever.

" From Acú I have a less gruesome account, which runs like this:

" They were making the world, and Anó, the coyote, wanted to see what they were doing, but the men did not want Anó to come near. So they ordered Koo-ee'-ho-nitch, the spider, to catch Anó. Then Koo-ee'-ho-nitch cast his webs very far to catch Anó, for he was not letting them make the world; but Koo-ee'-ho-nitch was not able to catch Anó with all his nets, and the coyote always escaped, and so he remained. Now, *las Siete Cabrillas* were seven girls who went about in the world, and the coyote wanted to marry one of them. One of the girls said, ' He is bothering us too much.' Then said another — Acú gave her name, as well as the names of her sisters, but they are so unpronounceable that I spare you them — then said this other, ' Let us go into the sky, it is better for us to go up to the sky.' So when Anó, the coyote, came to where the girls were, they were not there but up in the sky. Then Anó looked in the water and saw them like a picture. So Anó jumped at the water and fell in. Then said one of the girls, ' It is better to call him up here and let him be with us,' and they called down to him from above, but Anó said, 'I can't go up; how can I go up there?' So they let down a rope to him and he caught hold of it. Then they began to pull him up, saying all together to encourage him, *ho-te, ho-te, ja-le, ja-le*. At last, when Anó was near them, one of them said, 'All right now, cut the rope!' Then they cut the rope, and there in the sky Anó stays, always following after the sisters, and that star is called Anó, the coyote. It is a big star."

As the Father finished I stepped into the garden and scanned the sky. There in the eastern heavens twinkled the Pleiades, and following in their track was a bright star. I recognized it as Aldebaran, and Acú was right.

CHAPTER SEVEN

Of the Journey of Nahachis, and how he
Named the Places; and the Remarkable
Story of the Three Brothers Chico.

"LAST night I was telling you," said the Father the next evening, "Acú's account of the coyote's adventure with the Seven Sisters when the world was being made. Today I came upon the notes I made of a myth related to me by an Indian named Eustaquio, who lives not far from the mission with his wife Micaela. His people were not San Juaneños but mountain folk from beyond Pala. One day when he was here at the mission he told me how people first came into being, and the story of the great journey made by a certain Naháchis, when he gave names to many places of the land. And this is how Eustaquio told it, except that I will turn his Spanish into English if you prefer."

I did prefer, and the Father, opening one of his *libritos,* read as follows:

The *laguna* at Elsinore is the place where people first appeared in the world, and they called it Pai'yachee. It was not water then, but a *ciénaga,* swampy ground like mud. At first all was dark, always it was night; there was no sun, no light at all. Then of a sudden people were born of the earth, all together there in the dark. They came up out of the mud like ants crawling out of a hole, but aimlessly and slowly, feeling their way, for they could not see, membling to themselves, this way, that way, and eating mud to keep themselves alive. They were all crowded together, and most of them very stupid, *como animales,* like animals.

One of them, Temét, who was wiser, began to shine and throw light all about, and to cause others to cast their shadows on the ground. When the people saw the light shining near them faintly and caught sight of one another's shadows, they were frightened and cried out, " *hee-tá-ush* — here comes a devil." Then when Temét saw that he frightened the people, he went down into the earth again, and going far away began to rise in the east, and to light up the sky along the edge of the earth; and as he rose higher and higher, and grew brighter, the people pointed and said, "There is the sun rising!"

Then Naháchis, who was like a god among them, said: "See, he went alone, wishing to be the sun. Now it is my will that each of you may become what he wishes." So spoke *el que mandaba*, he who ruled; and he gave them their choice of becoming whatever they chose to be. Then one said "I want to be *moó-e-la*, the moon, and shine during the night." And he became the moon, and took his place in the sky and began to shine at night. Another said, "I want to become *shoo-la*, a star, and live in the sky and shine at night." Then others said, "We want to become *shoo-la-yem*, that is stars." So they, too, became stars. And another said, "I want to be *tó-a-ta*, a rock." But Naháchis said, "If you become a rock, they will break you." But he answered, "*No le hace*, no matter, I want to be a rock." So he became a rock. Another said, "I want to be *coo-lá-ut*, a tree." Then Naháchis said, "If you are a tree, they will chop you down and burn you." But he said, "No

matter, I want to become a tree," and he became
a tree. Another said, " I want to be *hung-la,* the
wind "; and another, " I want to be *pee-qua-la,*
a snake, and crawl on the ground." Then Naháchis said, " If you become a snake the people
will take sticks and kill you "; but he said, " *No
le hace,* no matter, I want to be a snake." So he
became a snake, and that is why the people kill
a snake whenever they see one. And another
said, " I want to be a *tow' shahet,* a rabbit." But
Naháchis said, " If you become a rabbit they
will chase and catch you and kill you and eat
you." But he said, " It makes no difference, I
want to be a rabbit," and so he became a rabbit.
And another said, " I want to be *shangai'la,* a
gull." But Naháchis said, " If you are a gull
you will eat fish (*omk kaiyu' mel quak'
mahan*)." But he said, " *No le hace,* I want to
be a gull."

Now, among the people were three who were
wiser — *mas vivo* — than the rest. They were
Temét, the sun; Tahquitch, the evil one; and
Naháchis, the good one, who was like a god
among them. Naháchis rose from the swamp;
but he did not say that he wanted to become an
animal or a tree or a stone; he said, " Poor peo-

ple, how long are they going to live? I shall
go a journey and name the places and return
here again, and then the people will live longer.
Now I go."

So he crawled out of the swamp and went
about giving names to places. And he arrived at
a place and called it Temecula, the same as the
people call it today. Then he went farther and
before entering the mountains, he came to another place and named it Pauba. Then farther
over that way he came to another place and
named it Pai'ha, because they gave him *pinole*
there made of *chia* into a broth like milk. This is
the place they now call Aguanga. From there he
went away and came to a place where there was
tule, or *tay'ish,* and he named it Tay'ish-pa, and
there they gave him *pinole* to eat with water.
Leaving Tay'ish-pa, he journeyed and came to
another place where the odor of hot water came
to his nostrils, and he called it Pala sha'kay-wit,
which is to say, Hot Water. It was a *rancheria*
of the Cahuilla tribe, and afterwards was called
Cupa, but people now call the place Warner's
Hot Springs.

Then he went on and turned around and
came back again; and coming to another place

he gave it a name and it is called La-ho'ya, because there is a hollow there. Farther this way, he came to another place and named it Yapeech'ee; and so to another, which he named Cuki; and still farther this way he reached a place which he named Wash'ha, where they gave him *pinole* of wild rice. From there he came to a place where the ground under his feet made a noise as he walked, and he said *paumá pamác* — "there is a noise here." So he named the place Pauma, as it is called to this day. From Pauma he went to another place beside a river and named it Pala, which means water, for here he was very thirsty and they gave him water to drink. Coming on in this direction he arrived at a place and named it Tumk, which is the same as we call Monserrate now. From there he came farther this way to a place where some girls were bathing; and it was hot. One of them was Wahow'kee, the toad; but she was *gente*, that is, people, too. She had very long hair and was the most beautiful of all; but when the wind blew her hair aside, and Naháchis saw that she had the form of a toad, he said something that made her angry and her relatives too. So they took the root of *chevnis*, which is the plant that is called *yerba del manso* in Spanish, and grinding it in a mortar they made mush of it and gave it to him to eat. And he fell ill from eating it; and as he continued on his journey back toward Pai'yachee he walked sick in the road; and when he reached Tak'shee, which is the place called Vallecitos now, a little valley where many rocks are between Fallbrook and Temecula, he died. And there he is yet in the shape of a stone, and if you like, padre, I will take you there and show you this stone, which was blessed many years ago by Padre Guillermo, whom people called Padre Blanco, because he wore a white gown, being a Dominican; and he named the stone José.

You see, Naháchis did not want to be the sun, the moon, a star, the wind, a cloud, a tree, a rabbit, nor any other thing, but wanted to give more life to the people. So he made the journey and gave names to the places. But because he did not finish the journey back to Elsinore, the people do not know how long they will live and so they have to die.

Upon concluding his story Eustaquio added this:

Down on the level floor of the valley toward

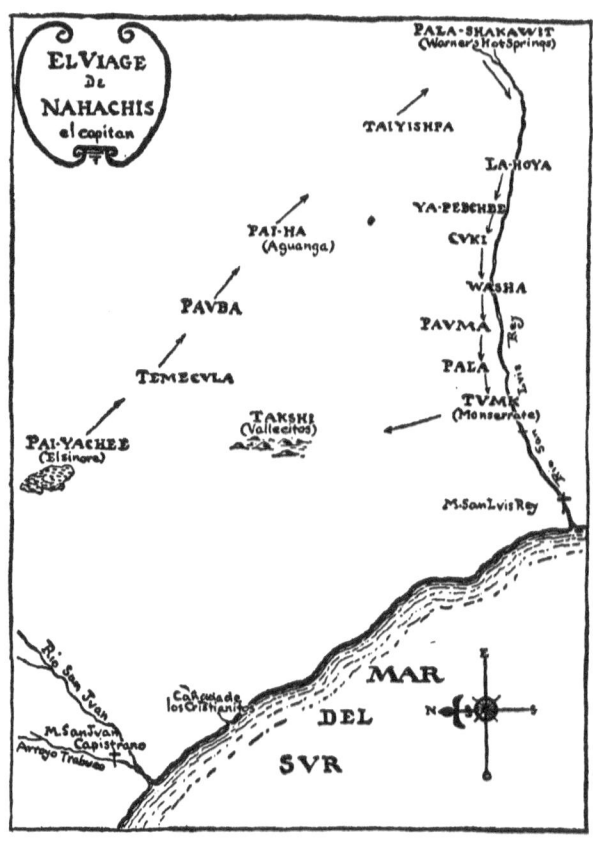

THE JOURNEY OF NAHACHIS

Temecula, the Indians used to grow grain. Sometimes in the hot summer, when the wheat was ripe and it happened that no breeze was stirring, they could not winnow the grain, because both grain and chaff would fall straight down together for lack of wind to blow the chaff away. Then they would send a messenger up to Naháchis to strike him gently with a stick or may be a small stone, and then the wind would begin to blow and the Indians could winnow the wheat.

" A strange story, truly, replete with aboriginal fancy and inconsequence," said I, as the Father closed the notebook. " It makes one realize that there is an Invisible California as yet undiscovered by the multitude, peopled with gods and demigods and mythologic heroes, and made memorable by their fanciful adventures. The next time I travel that region where Naháchis journeyed it will wear a new look to me. My thanks to Eustaquio and you."

" A different type of story," the Father proceeded, " is one that José Dóram, the Indian husband of Victoria, Acú's goddaughter, recently told. He said he heard it when a boy

while working in the San Matéo cañon, up toward La Cañada de los Cristianitos, about fifteen miles from here. That is believed to be the
spot where the padres, who were with Portolá
on his famous march in search of Monterey in
1769, baptized the dying Indian children — the
first Christian baptisms in California. The tale
is one of many the ranch hands used to tell in
the evenings to pass away the time, and is well
known among the old people. José is a sheep
shearer, and it is his custom to start out among
the southern California ranches in April, then
over to San Clemente Island, back to Bakers-
field and the San Joaquin, working his way
north through the sheep country of Nevada,
Utah, Wyoming and Montana, following his
vocation, and getting back home again at San
Juan Capistrano by the time the October rains
begin. He calls the story *Los Tres Hermanos
Chicos* — 'The Three Brothers Chico' — and
I will give it just as he told it to me."

Once there was a poor man named Francisco,
whose wife was Francisca and their three sons
were each named Francisco. Two of them were
grown men, but the youngest was still a boy, and

each was called Chico for short. One day the oldest went to his parents and asked for their blessing, saying that he wanted to go out into the world to look for adventure and to make money. Receiving their blessing he started out and presently arrived at a large house where an old man lived.

" Good afternoon, good grandfather," he said.

" Good afternoon, good youth," the old man answered, " and what are you doing in this land? "

Chico then said he was looking for work, and was told that he might stay all night and in the morning he would be given something to do. The next morning the old man addressed a letter to his mother and gave it to Chico to deliver, and at the same time furnishing him with a burro to ride and directions on the way. Some distance down the road Chico came to a wide river filled with alligators and all kinds of such animals, and with a large tree growing on the bank beside the road. On account of the dangers Chico decided he would not attempt to cross, and putting the letter up in the tree he sat down and waited for a few hours. Then he went back to the old man and reported that he had delivered the letter to the mother.

"Where is the answer?" inquired the old man.

"She was busy and said she would send the answer tomorrow," Chico replied.

"Very well," said the old man, "which will you have for your pay, *un talego de pesos ó un Diós-te-lo-pague* — a sack of money or a God-reward-you?"

"I'll have a sack of money," said Chico, and receiving it he went away.

Then one day the second Chico said to his parents that he also wanted to go out into the world in search of adventure and to make money. So they gave him their blessing and off he went. He too arrived at the old man's house, and after the same exchange of salutations as in his brother's case, he asked for work with the same result. After staying all night, he was given a letter to carry to the old man's mother, rode off on the burro, arrived at the river, was afraid to cross, put the letter into the same tree, sat down for several hours, and then returned to the old man telling him the same lies that his older brother had told.

" Very well," said the old man, " which will you have for your pay, a sack of money or a God-reward-you? "

" A sack of money," said Chico.

So the old man gave it to him and he went away.

Now the youngest brother Chico, seeing that his brothers were gone, wanted to go also, but his parents were at first unwilling, because he was so young. But after a while they gave their consent, and receiving their blessing he set out and also arrived at the house of the old man. Here he asked for work, was invited to stay all night, and in the morning was handed a letter to deliver to the old man's mother. This he put in the bosom of his shirt, and having been told what road to take, he was given a sheep to ride.

In a little while he arrived at the broad river full of alligators and all sorts of animals, but he was not afraid. Standing still for a moment and taking off his hat, he said " *Con Diós, mi amo* — with God, my master," and made the sheep plunge into the water and carry him to the other side. When he reached the other bank in safety he looked down and saw that only the feet of

the sheep were wet. " My horse is very large,"
he said. Then he gave thanks to God and trav-
eled on. It was not long before he came to another river, which was broad and black and
filled with the same kinds of animals as the first.
Chico stopped and saw that the road he was on
went down into the water, and coming out on
the other side continued straight ahead. So he
said, as before, " *Con Diós, mi amo*," and plung-
ing into the river with the sheep arrived safely
on the other side, where he gave thanks to God
and went on. Presently he reached a third broad
river, which was all red, because it was of blood.
It was filled, as were the first two, with alligators and all kinds of animals. He stood a moment, and seeing that the road here also went
straight on upon the opposite side, he said " *Con
Diós, mi amo*," and immediately rode into the
water on his sheep and came out safely on the
other bank.

Again giving thanks to God he continued on
his way, and soon there appeared ahead of him
two large swords crossing each other and moving
back and forth as if duellists were fighting with
each other across the road. The motion of the
swords was unceasing, but Chico stopped only a

moment and saying " *Con Diós, mi amo,*" urged his sheep through and giving thanks to God journeyed on. In a little while he saw ahead of him two *manos de metate*, stones used for grinding corn on a *metate*. They came at each other from opposite sides of the road, striking together over the center, then parting, continued to strike and part. When Chico saw these, he paused for a moment, but saying " *Con Diós, mi amo,*" he went ahead and passed without harm between the stones. Then giving thanks to God he proceeded on his way. Farther along he saw two mountains crash together in the road, withdraw to either side and crash again, and so continue. As before, Chico stopped, then said " *Con Diós, mi amo,*" and passed with the sheep in safety between the clashing mountains. Again giving thanks to God, he continued his journey. Next he came to a pasture with high grass that looked green and rich, and many sheep were in the pasture, but so thin they seemed to be dying. " In the name of God," said he, " why are the sheep dying of hunger in so rich a pasture? " Then, a little farther on, he came to another flock of sheep that were very fat in a place where there was no grass at all, and he said, " In the name of God, is it possible there is no grass here and such fat sheep? "

Finally, the young Chico arrived at a beautiful garden, like Paradise, where every flower that is known was growing, and in the garden was the house where the old man's mother lived, whom he soon saw standing at the door.

" *Buenas tardes, buena abuelita* — good evening, good little grandmother," said Chico.

" *Buenas tardes, buen niño* — good evening, good child," she answered.

" I bring you a letter from your son," said Chico, and handed her the letter.

Then she told him that he might let the sheep go to graze, and invited him to come into the garden and sleep. So he did and slept a whole year. When the old woman called him and said he had slept a long time he could hardly believe it, for he felt that he had been sleeping only an hour. Then she gave him a letter, which she said was the answer, and he should carry it back to the old man. The young Chico did not want to leave the garden, but she told him that he must go now but that he might return again. Thus the Virgin sent him back, for it was the

Virgin herself who lived in the house in the midst of the garden.

So he set out again, but whereas on his coming the road had been beset with great rivers, swords, stones, mountains, lean and fat sheep, none of these things were to be seen on the return — only a straight, level road which led directly to the house of the old man who was her son. He asked Chico why he had been so long, and Chico said he had slept an hour in the garden, but the old man told him he had been gone a year, and asked what he had seen upon the road. When Chico finished telling all that had happened the old man asked him if he knew what all these things were, and he said he did not. Then the old man explained them to him.

" The first broad river that you saw," said he, " was the milk that you took from your mother's breast; the second river, which was black, was hell with all the souls in it in the shape of animals; the third river, which was red, was purgatory with the souls who were doing penance in the form of animals; the swords that were crossing one another over the road were two *compadres* who had quarreled in this world and were

doing penance for it in the other world; the two
manos de metate that continually struck one
another across the road were two *comadres*[1]
who had quarreled in this world and were doing
penance for it in the other; the two mountains
that clashed across the road at intervals were a
pair who had lived without being properly married and were doing penance for it in the other
world; the rich pasture with the starving sheep
was envy; and the fat sheep where there was no
grass were the souls in heaven."

Then the old man asked,

" As a reward for what you have done, which
will you have, a sack of money or a God-reward-
you? "

And the young man replied that he would
have a God-reward-you; whereupon the old
man gave him a little rod and a little square
piece of cloth, and said,

" Whenever you want something, strike the
cloth with the little rod and say, ' *Barrita, barrita, por la virtud que Diós te ha dado, me des*

---

[1] When one stands as godfather or godmother for a
child at baptism, that person becomes the *compadre* or
comadre of the parents. The godfather is the *padrino* of the
child; the godmother is its *madrina*. The *compadres* or
comadres must never quarrel. Hence the penance in this case.

un tal cosa — little rod, little rod, by the power that God gave thee, give me so-and-so.' "

So Chico took the rod and cloth and putting them in the bosom of his shirt, started homeward.

On the road he fell in with the two older brothers, who were also on their way home after their adventuring. They asked him what he was taking home to their mother, and he answered, " a God-reward-you." They scolded him for not having taken money, and he asked them what they were bringing home. They answered, " Nothing," for indeed they had spent all their money. Thereupon they killed him and buried him by the roadside, and went on. Then the Virgin, who was the old woman who lived in the house in the garden, came and brought him to life again, so that he continued on his way home, and soon caught up with his brothers. They were surprised to see him and asked each other if they had not killed him. So they killed him again, and gathering together a great pile of wood, they put his body on top and burned it. But again the Virgin came, and gathering together his ashes with her hands brought him to life, so that he started on again and once more

caught up with his brothers. Again they killed
him, and this time they took his body and sank
it in a *laguna*. As he lay at the bottom of the
laguna, a stem grew out of his body and blossomed on top of the water into a beautiful and
fragrant flower. By and by, some *arrieros*, or
mule-drivers, passing that way with their mules,
saw the flower floating on the water, and it
looked so lovely that one of them waded into
the pond with his mule and plucked it. As he
proceeded on his way he put the flower to his
nose and mouth, and the flower immediately
spoke. " *Pítame, mi padre ó mi madre*," it said,
" *que mi hermano, Chico grande, y el segundo
me han matado* — repay for me, my father or
my mother, for my oldest brother Chico and
the second have killed me."

In surprise the *arriero* handed the flower to
one of his companions, who put it to his mouth.
The flower spoke the same words again and this
happened to all the company who put the flower
to their mouths. After a while they arrived at
the town where the Chicos lived, and when the
father and the mother had heard the flower
speak, it was offered to the two brothers, but for
them it would speak nothing at all. The neighbors then began to suspect that the two older

Chicos had killed their younger brother. Accordingly they all went to the *laguna* whither the *arrieros* led them, and the one who had plucked the flower pointing out the place, they raised the body from the water and it came to life and told all that had happened. The people then took the older Chicos and punished them as they deserved. The first thing that the little Chico did was to strike the square cloth with the rod and say,

"*Barrita, barrita, por la virtud que Diós te ha dado, dale á mi papa un caballo blanco* — little rod, little rod, by the virtue that God has given thee, give my father a white horse," which immediately appeared. Then for his mother he asked for some food.

For a little while Chico stayed with his parents, and then he began to long to go to the beautiful garden he had seen and stay with the Virgin. So he told his parents he was going, but not to mourn for him when he was gone, because they would soon follow him and be with him and the Virgin. Soon he died and not long after his death his father and mother followed him.

"*Es largo, pero aquí se acaba* — the story is long, but here it ends," said José.

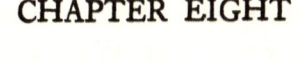
CHAPTER EIGHT

OF THE DAWN HYMN, CHILDREN'S PRAYERS
AND THE SONG OF THE WAKES. SOME PROV-
ERBS AND *DICHOS*.

ONE evening I asked the Father if the famous description in the novel *Ramona* of the Dawn Hymn was based on an actual custom.

"Surely," he replied, "that was one of the loveliest practices of Spanish California, the singing of *El Alba*, as they called the hymn. Doña Balbineda, who was born here in the mission building, says that her mother remembered how the rough voices of the soldiers in the *cuartel*, or guardhouse, could be heard joining in it just as day broke; and Doña María has told me that when she was a little girl on her father's ranch, it was the practice of the family to sing it every weekday morning *muy temprano*, as she expressed it, very early. At the first sign of light her father's voice resounded through the house, calling, ' *Levántense, muchachos, y asiéntense á rezar* — rise, children, and sit up to pray! ' Thereupon all the family would sit up in bed and repeat the angelus — *el ángel del Señor anunció a María* — and as soon as this was concluded the *alba* was started. There was no getting out of it; if any did not awake, they were made to awake; and the little María, who was the baby of the family, would thrust her head back into the pillow, immediately prayer and song were ended, for another nap. There are versions of the *alba* with as many as a dozen stanzas or even more, but Doña María's family used only three. She has given these to me just as she sang them when a child:

Ya viene el alba,
Rayando el dia,
Daremos gracias
Con alegría.

Now comes the dawn,
Breaking is day,
Let us give thanks
With joyfulness.

Nació María
> *Para consuelo*
De pecadores
> *Y luz de cielo.*

Mary was born
> For consolation
Of sinners
> And light of heaven.

Viva Jesús,
> *Viva María*
Viva tambien
> *La luz de dia!*

Praised be Jesus,
> Praised be Mary,
Praised be also
> The light of day! [1]

On Sundays there was substituted for the *alba* an *alabanza,* or hymn to the Virgin, sung in many stanzas, of which this is the first:

[1] There is a version in which the third and fourth lines of the first stanza read
> *Digamos todos Ave María!*
> Let us all say Hail, Mary!

Salve, Vírgen pura,
Salve, Vírgen madre,
Salve, Vírgen bella,
Reina Vírgen, salve!

Hail, Virgin immaculate,
Hail, Virgin mother,
Hail, Virgin beautiful,
Queen Virgin, hail!

While the Father was telling me of these
matters and humming the airs of the hymns, I
noticed that his faithful *ama de llaves,* or house-
keeper, was hovering about the doorway, and
at the conclusion of the *alabanza* she called to
him softly. He went out to her and after a moment returned, saying with an apologetic smile:

"I have not been very well today, and
Cándida thinks I am overdoing my strength by
sitting up longer. She may be right; so, if you
will excuse me, I think it will be best for me to
retire, and I will see you again tomorrow.
Meantime you may find entertainment in looking through these *libritos* " — handing me several from the desk — " and so, if you don't
mind, *adiós hasta mañana.*"

ELALBA

ALABANZA

CANCION en los VELORIOS

1. THE DAWN HYMN.
2. HYMN TO THE VIRGIN.
3. SONG AT THE WAKES.

Thus left to myself, I spent an hour or two culling out tidbits. Some of these on old customs carried on the spirit in which the evening had begun, and I will share them with you. Here is a prayer of the children, a Spanish counterpart of our " Now I lay me." It is credited to Doña María. " I always liked," she says, " to see them on their little knees, their little hands put together (*las manitas puestas*)."

> *Con Diós me acuesto,*
>   *Con Diós me levanto,*
> *Con la gracia de Díos*
>   *Y la del Espíritu Santo.*

> With God I lie down,
>   With God I arise,
> With the Grace of God
>   And the Holy Ghost's.

> *Quien benedició el cáliz*
>   *La noche y la cena*
> *Bendiga mi cama*
>   *Y a quien duerme en ella.*

> Who blessed the chalice
>   The night and the supper,

Bless my bed
  And who sleeps in it.

A mi cama de canto á canto
  Que no llegue cosa mala
Mas que Diós
  Y el Espíritu Santo.

To my bed from edge to edge
  Let no evil come,
Only God
  And the Holy Ghost.

And in the morning was this version:

Con Diós me acuesto
  Con Diós me levanto
Con la gracia de Diós
  Y el Espíritu Santo.

With God I lie down,
  With God I arise,
With the Grace of God
  And the Holy Ghost.

La Vírgen me tape
  Con el velo y con su manto,
Sin que nadie me tiente,
  Solo Diós y el Espíritu Santo.

The Virgin cover me
  With veil and her mantle,
So nobody may touch me,
  Only God and the Holy Ghost.

There were many forms of grace before and after meals. I like the inclusiveness of this one:

Thanks I give thee, O great Lord, for the food thou givest me though I do not merit it, and may the souls in purgatory rest in peace. Amen.

(*Gracias te doy, O gran Señor, por el sustento que me das aunque yo no lo merezco, y que las ánimas del purgatorio descansen en paz. Amen.*)

Of dramatic interest I found the Song of the Wakes, sung at the *velorios,* or wakes over the body of the dead — a custom still observed at San Juan. The room in which the coffin rests is cleared of furniture, the walls adorned with holy pictures, flowers, drapery of old laces and so on, and around the edges of the room chairs are placed for the mourners. These are invariably occupied by women, the men congregating about the door and mostly outside, where a blazing fire is kept up all night, for Capistrano nights even in summer are quite cool. All night long the mourners remain, joining from time to time in reciting the rosary as well as singing the song that follows below, until finally at the first appearance of light in the east, *El Alba,* the Dawn Hymn, is begun. The vividness of the Spanish original is but poorly reflected, I am afraid, in my literal translation.

Cancion en los Velorios

I

Orillas de un ojo de agua
Estaba un ángel llorando,
De.ver que se condenaba
El alma que tenía á su cargo.

Song at the Wakes

I

At the edge of a spring was an angel weeping, to see forever damned the soul he had in charge.

II

La Vírgen le dice al ángel:
No llores, ángel varon,
Que yo alcanzaré con mi hijo
Que esta alma alcanze perdon.

II

Says the Virgin to the angel: Weep not,
man angel, I will obtain from my Son for
this soul a pardon.

III

Hijo querido llamado,
Hijo de mi corazón,
Por la leche que mamastes
Que esta alma alcanze perdón.

III

O Son called beloved, Son of my heart, by
the milk of my breasts let this soul receive
pardon.

IV

Madre querida llamada,
Madre de mi corazón,

Como quieres que perdone
Si en tanto nos ofendió?

IV

O Mother called beloved, Mother of my heart, why askest thou pardon for so great offender?

V

Hijo querido llamado,
Hijo de mi corazón,
Pastoreando sus ovejas
Un rosario me rezó.

V

O Son called beloved, Son of my heart, shepherding his sheep a rosary he prayed me.

VI

Madre querida llamada,
Madre de mi corazón,
Si tanto quieres est' alma
Pues sacala de ese ardor.

VI

O Mother called beloved, Mother of my heart, since thou lovest this soul so, pluck it from the flame.

VII

La Vírgen como piadosa
Al infierno se arrojó
Con su santo 'scapulario
De la mano lo sacó.

VII

The Virgin all pitying descended to hell, with her holy scapulary she snatched up the soul.

VIII

Sale el diablo envenenado
Para los cielos tiró:
Señor, el alma que me has dado
Tu madre me la quitó.

VIII

Went the devil envenomed and came near to heaven: Lord, the soul thou didst give me Thy mother has robbed me of.

IX

Quítate de aquí, Lucifer,
  Tu no eres mas de un traidor,
Pues lo que mi madre hiciera
  Por bien hecho lo doy yo.

IX

Away from here, Lucifer, thou art no more
than a traitor, what my mother would do as
done I vouchsafe her.

X

  Los ángeles en el cielo
  Toditos á una voz:
  El Señor nos dé la gloria
  Como se la dió al pastor.

X

The angels in heaven all with one voice:
" The Lord grant us glory as He granted
the shepherd! "

XI

  El rosario de María
  No lo dejes de rezar,

Es el primer escalón
Que al cielo hemos de llegar.

XI

The rosary of Mary fail not to pray, it is
the first step on the heavenly stair.

The Father's notebooks revealed *adivinan-*
zas, or riddles, as a favorite scource of entertainment in old San Juan. Many of these are of a
punning nature in the Spanish; so that the point
is lost in translation.[1] Others are not so dependent on a play of words; for example, this: What
does a shepherd in the field see that neither the
Pope in Rome nor the king of Castile on his
throne can see? Another shepherd. (*Que ve un*
pastor en el campo que ni el Papa en Roma ni el
Rey de Castilla en su trono puede ver? Otro
pastor.)

And then the proverbs — they fairly bristled
from the pages.

There is an adage in California to the effect
that the proverbs and sayings of the old Spanish
people are little gospels — *evangelios chiquitos.*

---

[1] For example: *Cuantas son las estrellas?* that is, How
many are the stars? And the answer is, *Cincuenta,* fifty; but
this word is pronounced by Spanish Californians as though it
were *sin cuenta,* which means " without number."

In San Juan the speech of the inhabitants is well seasoned with such Hispanic salt. Some of these *dichos, refranes,* or sayings, such, for instance, as " they went for wool and came back shorn," and another about the folly of looking for three feet on the cat, persist in the very words Cervantes put into Sancho Panza's mouth over three centuries ago. Others are of a more local flavor, or perhaps they have been brought up from Mexico, the mother of Spanish California; but local though they be, the humor of them has a universal appeal. This one for instance:

> *La cana engaña,*
> *El diente miente,*
> *La ropa pone en duda,*
> *Pero rastrar los piés*
> *Es así que es vejez;*

which I have amused myself by Englishing as follows:

> Gray hairs may be liars,
> Failing teeth may deceive,
> You're not sure you are old
> Though ragged the sleeve;
> But when the feet drag,
> You've got to believe!

Society's tendency to excuse in the rich what it condemns unsparingly in the poor is hit off in this quatrain:

Cuando el pobre se emborracha
Y el rico en su compañia,
La del pobre es borrachera
Y del rico es alegría.

When the poor man gets befuddled
With the rich to share his folly,
The poor man's case is drunkenness,
The rich man is just jolly.

No hay cuña mas mala que la del propio palo, "no wedge is worse than one from the same tree," is a manner of saying that nobody can be meaner to you than one of your own family. *Despues del conejo ido, pedradas al matorral,* "after the rabbit is gone stone the bush," is, of course, only another way of telling us to lock the stable after the horse is stolen. *Cada venida del obispo,* "at each coming of the bishop," is the equivalent of that modern saying of ours, once in a blue moon. Our blunt Anglo-Saxon " out of sight out of mind " is more gracefully expressed

as *ojos que no miran, corazón que no siente,*
" eyes that do not see, heart that does not feel."
Nadie sabe que tanto pesa el muerto hasta que
carga las andas, " nobody knows how heavy the
corpse is until he carries the bier," alludes to the
old custom of the bearers at funerals carrying
the body to the grave on foot — a custom still
prevailing in parts of California, where, as at San
Juan, it is a long way to an undertaker and his
hearse. *Como el Apache viejo, no mata pero*
hace jaras, " like the old Apache, he does not
kill, but he makes arrows," warns us that the rul-
ing passion may persist even in age. *El que entre*
lobos anda á aullar se enseña, " who runs with
wolves is taught to howl," is a homely version of
evil communications corrupting good manners.
And there is that other *dicho* which hits off the
case of the thief who remains a thief in spite of
punishment: *Perro queda en comer huevos*
aunque le quemen el hocico; that is, " the dog
keeps on eating eggs though they burn his
snout." I enjoy, too, the quaint tit-for-tat of an
old saying of Doña María's: Said the geese to
the swallow, " *Adiós,* crazy swallows, you come
a few and you go away a many." Said the swallows to the geese, " *Adiós,* foolish geese, you

come a many and you go away a few " (because, you see, the people kill the geese).

But to return to our poets. Town dwellers, particularly in congested districts, will certify, I am sure, the soundness of the advice extended in the following verses:

> *Cantar bien ó cantar mal*
> *En el campo es diferente,*
> *Pero delante de la gente*
> *Cantar bien ó no cantar.*

> Sing well or sing ill
> In the country no matter,
> But where there are people
> Sing well or keep still.

And here is one from Doña Rafaela, which has doubtless come up from Mexico where loquats are little esteemed, being mostly skin and stone, unless well cared for:

> *Quien nísperas come y bebe cerveza*
> *Espárragos chupa y besa una vieja,*
> *Ni come, ni bebe, ni chupa, ni besa.*

Who eats loquats and drinks beer, sucks asparagus and kisses an old woman, neither eats, nor drinks, nor sucks, nor kisses.

Every old California settlement has its clumps of *nopal*, the flat-jointed prickly pear cactus, whose fruits, called *tunas*, are greatly relished by Mexicans and Indians, and it is not surprising to find it the inspiration of several *dichos*, as this:

> *Ingratas, crueles fortunas;*
> *Acabo de conocer*
> *Que al nopal vienen á verlo*
> *Solo cuando tiene tunas;*
> *Menos, ni se acuerdan de él.*

Thankless, cruel fortune;
  I have come to know
They only visit the nopal
  When the tunas show;
Without, it is not even held in mind.

The Franciscan Fathers brought up from Mexico two large-fruiting species of *nopal* and planted hedges of them about the missions. The children of San Juan have a pretty rhyme in which the *tuna* plays a part, associated with the moon's reflection in the waters of a pond:

> *Allá está la luna*
> *Comiendo su tuna*

Y tirando las cáscaras
En la laguna

There is the moon
Eating her tuna
And throwing the rind
In the laguna.

And a deal of truth as well as patient philosophy
is, I fear, embodied in these four lines:

Es que una vez un Indio
Perdió su zapeta;
Y dijo, " el que tiene pierde,"
Y quedó en pelota!

There was once an Indian
Lost his breech clout;
Said he, " who has must lose,"
And remained without!

As a final touch I want to set down a saying
attributed in the Father's notes to Acú, though
it took Doña María to clear up the point of it.
" *Música pagada toca mal son,*" remarked Acú,
" paid music makes a bad sound." And Doña
María's enlightening comment upon it was,
" You see, when they are paid beforehand they

are already paid, the musicians, and they don't make good music, because they are already paid."

I was telling the Father afterwards of my discoveries among his proverbs and *dichos*, and he observed:

" Apropos of that saying *á cada venida del obispo*, or, as we would say, once in a blue moon, I recall a certain humorous little happening of which they tell as occurring in the eighteen fifties. You must know that when the bishop did come, it was customary to receive him with very elaborate preparations — the ringing of bells, the firing of the little cannon known as *camaras*, and other demonstrations of gladness. On this particular occasion the bishop was expected to arrive from the south for confirmation, and the people of the pueblo had spent days in happy anticipation of the great event, making arches of willow poles bound together with rawhide and decorated with greenery and flowers of colored paper.

" On the morning of the day he was due everybody turned out to install the arches at equal distances along the *camino real*, the King's Highway, which approaches the mission from the south and along which the bishop was assumed to be traveling, since he was coming up from San Luis Rey. The people lined the road as far as the arches extended, gazing hopefully southward, each eager to catch the first glimpse of the bishop and his party, who were of course expected to pass beneath the triumphal arches on their way to the mission. Suddenly, while every eye was strained towards the south, an excited messenger appeared from the west side of the valley with the disconcerting news that the bishop was not arriving by the *camino real* at all, but was coming by a different road up the west side of the valley and was even then very close to the mission. The word quickly passed from mouth to mouth, and an exodus from the *camino real* began at once, everyone hastening to greet the bishop over on the west road. But the arches, the triumphal arches that had cost so many days of patient labor — were they to be abandoned? *De ningun modo,* by no means. Ready hands tore them from their footings, and the crowd bore them pell mell across the fields to the Trabuco road, and arriving in the very nick of time held them in place by hand, while the bishop made his entry through them to the joy and satisfaction of all."

CHAPTER NINE

Of the Arroyo Trabuco and some Pleasant Tales that Haunt it. Of Crisanta's
Cazo and how its Handles became Horseshoes. The Story of the Ungrateful Alligator and how the Coyote Lost Faith
in Man.

T H A T section of San Juan which lies to the west of the railroad tracks is particularly alluring to me because of a little row of wooden dwellings with back yards sloping down to the flat that skirts the Arroyo Trabuco. Trabuco, by the way, means a blunderbuss. One of the soldiers of Portolá's famous expedition up the California coast in 1769 in quest of the port of Monterey, lost a weapon of the sort somewhere along the banks of this stream, an event of so much importance as to be chronicled in the diary of the party. The loss was the little river's gain, for thus it got its name. It is a pretty stream, issuing in the dimpled *lomas* to the north, and on reaching the valley flows past half-recumbent, century-old sycamores to join the San Juan a little below the village, and so to the ocean two miles farther on. Today the Trabuco's lower reaches are thickly hedged with willows and *guatamote*, but in former years, the *ancianos* say, it was not so, and one sitting in the mission corridor of a clear day could see its waters running open in the sun, and at the vista's end the white surf lapping on the beach.

But the Trabuco has other associations than that of the lost blunderbuss. There is, for instance, the tradition of the musical cliffs far up the cañon from which, they say, mysterious melodies would issue just at sunset — sweet harmonies as of violin and flute and drum. Many of the old people have testified to hearing the music, but never one can say who made it.

Trabuco legend, however, has mostly to do with buried treasure. It has already been narrated how the padres of San Juan transported their belongings and hid them for a time in the Trabuco cañon, while the Argentinian *insurgentes* were looting the coast something over a century ago. That, in itself, was enough to make the little stream and its borders the fruitful scene of hidden treasure tales. One of these has

an unusual dénouement. In old times, it seems,
a few *rancheros* lived in the cañon, and one of
the ranch houses, long since deserted and fallen
into ruin, belonged, they say, to Juan Erroque,
a Basque who had sheep. One day, Manuel
Sales, an Indian from Pala, came riding up the
cañon on a lively horse, *un caballo muy bravo*.
He tied his animal to a post outside the house
while he went about the business that brought
him there. During his absence the horse jerked
its head and pulled out the post, and when Manuel returned, there was the hole with a thousand pesos at the bottom of it. He did not touch
the money, for it was not his, you see; but when
Erroque returned, Manuel told him about it,
which was no news to Erroque, for, it transpired,
he himself had put it there!

Then there is the case of José Juan who, when
a lad, used to work in the Trabuco for a Portuguese. One evening he was told to drive the
cattle far up into the hills to browse until morning and as he was going along with them he
came to an old adobe house — an ancient house,
half ruined, with thick walls and a remnant of
tiled roof, and it may have been that very house
of Juan Erroque's though this is but conjecture.

And as he would have passed it, his attention was caught by the sight of a light within, which was strange, for the house was evidently deserted. So José Juan crept up to a window and peeped in to see if the building might not be on fire. But no; all that could be seen was a single flame in a corner of one room, flaring up to the ceiling and then sinking down to the floor — *subiendo y bajando* — the familiar sign of hidden treasure. So, when the light at last disappeared, José Juan took out his knife and going into the room he made a cross-mark on the wall exactly where he had seen the flame arise and descend. Then he hastened back to report the matter to the Portuguese, who took José Juan and immediately went up the cañon to the house, and the two dug and delved at the marked spot until at breast-deep they uncovered an olla with a narrow mouth which was closed with a plug of sycamore wood. Upon removing this they found the jar full of gold money, old-fashioned, angular pieces called *onzas esquinadas*. José Juan's eyes glistened, though not because of the gold, for he was an Indian. What I want, said he, is the olla. But unluckily, as they lifted it out, the olla fell into a hundred pieces; and though, when pressed by the Portuguese, he took a few coins home for his father, the latter scolded him for a thief and forced him to return the money to his master. So poor José Juan had nothing but trouble for his discovery, and as for the Portuguese he soon quit the Trabuco and was never heard of again.

Simple, honest tales these, that put no bad taste in the mouth and are in keeping with the tranquil beauty of the arroyo that is their stage. Almost do they convert me in their innocence to the reality of those melodious cliffs.

But I am wandering far from that part of San Juan beyond the railroad tracks of which I started out to speak. It is a picturesque neighborhood inhabited by families of the laboring class, where garden flowers of old California peep through the palings and loll beside the unkempt paths — lilies of Mary, marvel of Peru, hollyhocks, marigolds and nasturtiums, the flower of the twisted nose. It is informing to chat with the old señoras who tend them, and who know them by names that often preserve a tidbit of romance. It was so that I first heard the French marigold called *cempasuchil,* a pure Aztec word that whisks the fancy back to Montezuma and

the gardens of pre-Columbian Mexico, where it
bloomed long before the coming of the Con-
quistadores. And hollyhocks — a meaningless
term to us — is called in San Juan *la vara de
San José*, that is Saint Joseph's staff, whose five
short words embody a pretty legend which
Doña María told me. " When it was that the
Blessed Virgin," said she, " should have a husband, many came to sue for her, but she was to
accept only that one whose staff would break
into flower when he came. So when Saint Joseph
came, his staff blossomed up and down its
length just as the flower in our gardens
does today, and so Saint Joseph's staff it is
called."

One evening I was speaking to the Father
about this old quarter of San Juan and he remarked:

" It was over there that Crisanta lived, the
old Indian woman who told the story of Matilda, you remember. Near a fence post at the
rear of her place I noticed, one day, a heavy,
circular, copper vessel like a kettle, some twenty
inches in diameter, with two old horseshoes
riveted on the rim for handles.

" ' Crisanta,' I asked, ' what is this? '

" ' Padre,' she replied, ' that is a *cazo* for cooking food, but we don't use it any longer. Los 'mericanos nowadays sell us tin pans to use on the stove.'

" And was this kettle of the Mission, I wanted to know?

" ' It was, padre. When the great *temblor* came and killed the Indians in the church, there were many little orphans left — *muchos huerfanitos.* They were then gathered into one house and this old *cazo* was used for cooking their *frijoles* and *posole*, their beans and hominy. Then when the children grew up and the *cazo* was not needed for them any longer, it was left in our family. See the poor horseshoes instead of the pretty handles of *bronce* it used to have. One time a hole came in the bottom where you see that patch, and we took it to the American blacksmith to have the hole fixed, and when it came back the good bronze handles were gone and these old rusty horseshoes were there instead. *Qué americano* — ah, those Americans! ' "

" I suppose we cannot deny the justice of the uncomplimentary implication," said I, " if what we hear of the roguery and sharp practice of the first Americans in California is true, or half true."

" Did I ever tell you the story of the ungrateful *caiman*, or alligator? " inquired the Father, by way of answer.

He had not, so, at my request, he continued:

" The land holdings of the Spanish Californians under Mexico were in many cases nothing short of princely, and had they been kept intact until the present day would have made the family descendants millionaires many times over. The tale of how the properties were lost to the original owners is sometimes anything but creditable to those who acquired them. The old-time Californians neither asked nor gave notes when money, cattle or other property was loaned. Their word was sufficient, for it was a point of honor to keep it. ' The Californians had *vergüenza* (shame) in them,' observed one possessor of a proud old name to me. ' They thought more of their promise than of the *peso*. *El dinero*, they would say, *va y viene y la amistad en su lugar* — money goes and comes, friendship stays in its place.' So when the *extranjeros* arrived — that is, the outsiders, who were mostly Americans and keen for a bargain

— the Californians in their simplicity thought their word good too, befriended them and trusted them only to find, too often, the act of faith taken advantage of. Apropos of such treacherous doings there is current in San Juan this Story of the Ungrateful Alligator."

Once there was an alligator lying on the bank of a pond, *boca arriba,* that is, on its back with its mouth up, and all tangled up with *sargazo,* or seaweed; and when alligators are so, with their feet up, they cannot turn themselves over, *de ningun modo,* by no means. They have to stay where they are unless some one turns them over. And there was a man passed by there and he said, " The poor alligator, he is going to die if I don't put him in the water." So he took him and carried him to the water. He went into the water up to his knees, with the alligator on his shoulders. " Put me further in," said the alligator; and the man went until the water was above his middle. " Further in, still," cried the alligator, and the water was up to the man's neck. Then the alligator caught the man with his claws and said, " Now, I shall eat you. I am very hungry." And the man said, " God bless me, didn't I save your life? If I had not put you in the water you would have died." Then said the alligator, " Don't you know that a good turn is paid by a bad one? " " Well," said the man, " here comes an old horse, let's ask him." So when the horse came up to them the man said, " Listen, brother horse, is it true that a good turn is paid by a bad one? " " Yes," said the horse, " that's true. When I was young my owners had me in a stable. I carried them wherever they wanted to go and they took good care of me; and now that I am old they turn me out to die." Then said the alligator, " Ah, you see! Now I am going to eat you." Then said the man, " No, just wait. There comes an old ox, let's ask him." So, when the ox reached the pond, the man said to him, " Tell me, brother ox, is it true that a good turn is paid by a bad one? " " Yes," said the ox, " it is true. When I was young my owners took good care of me. They fed me well so I could work and plough, but now that I am old they have cut off my horns and shorn me of my tail, and have turned me into the country to fatten, and then they will kill me." Then said the alligator again to the man, " Ah, you see! Now I am going to eat you."

THE MAN, THE ALLIGATOR AND THE COYOTE

Then the man became very sad and said to the
alligator, "Wait, this is the last favor I'll ask
of you. Here comes a coyote. If he says the same
as the others, then eat me." When the coyote
came trotting up, his tongue hanging out, the
man said to him, "Say, brother coyote, is it true
that a good turn is paid by a bad one?"
"What?" said the coyote. "Come away from
the water, I cannot hear for the noise of the
waves." Then the man repeated the question.
"Is it true that a good turn is paid by a bad
one?" "*Á segun* — that depends," said the coyote; and then said, "Why?" Then the man
said to him, "This alligator wants to eat me."
And the coyote said to him again, "Why?"
"This alligator," said the man, "was lying at
the edge of the pond, mouth up, and you know
that an alligator can never turn himself over,
and as I passed that way he put me up such a
whimper that I took and put him in the water,
and as soon as he found he was in the water he
turned on me with his claws and said, ' Now, I
am going to eat you.'" Said the coyote, "Well,
I cannot decide this question until you take him
and show me just how he was." The alligator
agreed to being taken and put as he was, and so

the man carried him and put him on his back,
feet up, in just the same position they had found
him in at first. Then said the coyote to the man,
" Leave him for an ingrate, and never do another favor to any alligator! "

Then the man turned to the coyote and said,
" How can I ever repay you, *coyotito*, for the
great favor you have done me? " " You have
that at home which will repay me," said the
coyote. " Then come to my house and get
it," said the man. " No," replied the coyote,
" because you have those there that say ' bow-
wow '; but you also have chickens; bring me
some of those. I'll wait for you here." So the
man went home, and in a little while returned with two chickens in his hand and a sack
over his shoulder. Then he let the chickens go,
and the coyote snapped them up. The man then
swung down the sack from his shoulder, and
said, " How will you have these, one at a time
or all in a heap (*una á una ó á montones*)? "
" All in a heap," said the coyote, " there won't
many escape me." " There they are! " cried the
man, and opening the sack he let out a pack of
hounds, which took after the coyote. The coyote
leaped through the tules and up to the top of a

loma, where he stopped and looked back at the man. " Come down," called the man, " I was only playing." At this the coyote got angry and shouted, " Playing, your foot! Hereafter, neither to my father nor my mother, nor my grandfather nor my grandmother, nor my great-grandfather nor my great-grandmother will I do a favor all the days of my life! "

CHAPTER TEN

How Acú Finished with the Month. The
Mission Swallows and how they Arrive
every Year for the Feast of Saint Joseph.

 TWO or more years elapsed before I was at the mission again. It was the time of the full moon, and after supper I strolled over to the ruined stone church and sat down upon a broken wall to indulge my fancy in this spot of tragic memory; for beautiful as the ruin is at any hour, it yields up a special loveliness at the touch of the moonlight. Californians have an engaging habit of giving ambitious names to their landmarks and scenery, and in my first days in the Golden State I was accustomed to hearing San Juan Capistrano called "The Melrose of the West," and was enjoined, if I would view it aright, to go visit it by the pale moonlight. I must leave it to those who have seen

Melrose under such conditions to judge of the worth of the comparison; but whatever that judgment, I am safe in saying that Capistrano's charm needs no such crutch to support it; every month the moon blesses the ancient pile with a mystical beauty that is sufficient of itself.

As I sat in placid contemplation of the scene, I heard steps approaching. It was the Father. He, too, enjoys the moonlit glories of his mission, and in a few moments he joined me on my bit of wall. After a while I spoke to him of the swallows' mud nests that line the broken cornices of the ruin, and how upon my visit years before I had been touched by their existence in such a spot. He then told me how it happens that so many are there.

" One day several years ago," he said, " I was passing the new hotel at the west side of the town plaza, and there was the proprietor out with a long pole smashing the swallows' nests that were under the eaves. The poor birds were in a terrible panic, darting hither and thither, flying and screaming about their demolished homes.

" What in the world are you doing? " I asked.

"'Why,' said he, 'these dirty birds are a nuisance, and I am getting rid of them.'

"'But where can they go?' I continued.

"'I don't know and I don't care,' he replied, slashing away with his pole, 'but they've no business here, destroying my property.'

"'Then come on, swallows,' I cried, 'I'll give you shelter. Come to the mission, there's room enough there for all!'

"Sure enough, they took me at my word, and the very next morning they were busy building under the eaves of the restored sacristy of Father Serra's church. By the way, there is a rather odd fact about these swallows. You know, they migrate every autumn, but their return is with the greatest regularity on Saint Joseph's day, the nineteenth of March. Within a few days they set about patching up their broken nests, building new ones and disputing possession of others with such vagrant sparrow families as may have taken up illegal quarters there during the swallows' absence. On this fragment of broken adobe wall, remains of the futile attempt to rebuild the stone church long ago, you will see them pecking the soil and with a great flutter of wings carrying it off as building material. They fly with it to the old mission *laguna* off there to the northeast of the buildings, and with water make a paste of the earth in their little beaks, amid more fluttering of wings at the pond's edge. Then a straight course to the mission's eaves to deliver their loads of mud plaster for the walls of their inverted houses, and receive the noisy congratulations of their mates. By the way, have I ever told you what Acú once said about the habits of these swallows? "

" No, you never did," I replied, " and how is Acú?"

" You did not know, then, that Acú is dead? " he returned. " I must tell you at once about that, for there was something remarkable in his last days. To make the account complete, let me go back a little. One day in the year nineteen-sixteen he was at the *campanario* tolling the two large bells, which bear the names San Vicente and San Juan. Ruperto *el güero* had died a few minutes before and the tolling was to announce the death. After a final loud clang of both bells at once, followed after a short interval by two more in quick succession — so indicating that it was a man who had died and not a woman or child — Acú hung the rope ends upon an iron spike in the *cam-*

panario wall and came slowly towards me, where I stood beside Father Serra's monument.

"'Acú,' I called to him.

"'*Mande, padre* — command me, Father,' he replied promptly, this being his usual form of response when I addressed him.

"'Acú, would you toll for me if I were to die?'

"'*Con mucho gusto, padre* — with much pleasure, Father,' he assured me with enthusiasm; and it was thereupon agreed between us that whichever died first, he or I, the other would *doblar* — that is, toll the passing bell.

"Now, Acú did beautiful work in rawhide, such as reins and head-stalls for horses, as examples in the mission museum will testify. His workshop was his own yard, where, in the shade of a pepper tree and a mission grapevine, the only large one remaining in San Juan, he would stake out the hides on the ground to dry, and then cut them round and round to produce the long narrow strips of *cuero* of which the *riendas,* or reins, were woven. Always a customer or two — or for that matter, three or four — were waiting on Acú to finish the set that had been promised perhaps a year before.

"But the years rolled on and Acú was getting old; and by ninteen-twenty-four he was complaining that he could not see very well, that he got dizzy — *atarantado*, as he termed it. When June came he was observed to become unusually busy. He was working on a set of *riendas* for his old *patrón* and *amigo*, Lewis Moulton, of El Toro and the Nigüel ranch. There, about the Fourth of July, Acú appeared, all decked out in a clean shirt and his long-tailed coat, to deliver the completed work.

"'Here,' said he, 'are the *riendas* I promised you. And now, goodbye, *patrón*, for in one month more there will be no more Acú.'

"The next day he came up to the mission, and to everyone he repeated the same farewell. '*Adiós*, pretty soon no more Acú.'

"His premonition was true; for soon he fell ill, and I gave him the Sacraments. I went to see him again on the twenty-eighth of July, and after leaving him, his goddaughter Victoria followed me out to the pepper tree.

"'Padre,' she said, 'a curious thing: My uncle Acú asked me this morning "what date is this?" and I by mistake told him it was the twenty-ninth. "That can't be," he said, "it must be the twenty-eighth, because there are still four days." *Qué curioso!* how strange! Is he, do you think, going to finish with the month? '

"Strange indeed; for on the thirty-first, shortly before five o'clock in the afternoon, word was brought me that Acú was gone. I hastened to toll his passing bell, so fulfilling the compact we had made eight years before.

" Acú had finished with the month."

After a pause, the Father went on:

" But I started to tell you what Acú had to say about the swallows — *golondrinas,* as he called them. We were standing some years ago, he and I, under the big pepper tree in the garden, talking about the feast of Saint Joseph, which would be the next day. It would be Acú's feast day too (for he was José de Gracia Cruz) and my birthday. 'Mass tomorrow morning,' I had just told some children, 'will be at a quarter past eight. No, it is not a holy day of obligation.'

" ' Yes, it is,' Acú put in, ' yes, it is; it is my feast day.'

" After a while he announced to me that he would keep his feast day by doing no work and going to mass. He then turned his eyes upward,

searched the sky in every direction, and finally
said in a half disappointed way,

" ' They haven't come yet, and tomorrow is
the day.'

" We were expecting the swallows to arrive
as usual for the feast of Saint Joseph and occupy
their mud houses along the cornices of the
church.

" ' But they always do come,' he added con-
fidently. ' They say, padre, that when they go
away from here at the summer's end, they fly
to Jerusalem and stay there through the winter.
I don't know why, but that is what people say —
así dicen; and after that, they come back here
again for the feast of Saint Joseph, and to build
their little houses in the mission.'

" ' But, Acú,' said I, ' between here and Jerusalem is a great ocean. How can they fly so far
without getting tired and falling into the
water? '

" ' You see, padre,' he replied very deliberately, ' they carry with them in their beaks a
little twig of a tree, and when they get tired
flying across the ocean they put the twig on the
water and alight upon it and rest themselves.
And do you know, padre, the swallows do not

work on Sunday? It is true. I have watched them, and on Sunday they all stay inside their houses and don't do any work at all. I have always wondered how it is they know when it is Sunday.'

" The next morning Acú was waiting for me when I came down to open the church. He had his good coat on, and went immediately into the church to await mass. The sacristy of the big stone church was then in use, and as I passed vested across the little patio behind the bells on my way to the side door of the sanctuary I noticed a bird dart overhead, but could not make out whether it was an eave-swallow or one of the white-throated swifts that live in the cracks of the sanctuary dome. I was not long in doubt, however, for during mass I was distracted by the noise of fluttering wings out in the little patio and the unmistakable squeaking cry of the eave-swallows. They had come for *la fiesta de San José*, and were just in time for mass. One of them, indeed, flitted through the church, the server boy informed me as I reëntered the sacristy after mass was over.

" And Acú was *muy contento* that the *golon-drinas* had arrived for his feast. ' Did I not tell you?' said he. Doña Balbineda, too, was delighted, as she stopped in the *portal* to draw her shawl about her shoulders.

"'Padre,' she called laughingly, 'they have arrived, the swallows!'"

EPILOGUE

So ends our little book. Most of the people whose sayings and stories are herein faithfully set down have passed into the life beyond, and in a few more years all will have gone and their memories with them. Fragmentary as are many of these *morceaux*, they hold the atmosphere of a period in California history that is tinged for us with romance, a period precious in our annals and one that we do not want to have forgotten. In garnering them Father O'Sullivan harvested better than he perhaps realized at the time; for quite undesignedly the collection fits in with the work of restoring his mission's outward lines by recalling and fixing in the written word somewhat of the hidden life that was San Juan Capistrano's two or three generations ago.

C. F. S.